Praise for CodeSkull

"*CodeSkull* is like a warm, nostalgic hug from your PS1 and old Goosebumps favorites. A quick, heartfelt read that is so much fun!"

—Tatiana Schlote-Bonne, author of
Such Lovely Skin

"If you were that kid who had light-up shoes and a backpack full of Goosebump paperbacks, *CodeSkull* is the throwback you need! This novella is jam packed with 90s nostalgia, action, and tech horror that will make you think twice about every gadget around you. I was gripped from start to finish. *CodeSkull* might have just come out of a time capsule buried in a 90's playground. Put this on the shelf next to R.L. Stine and Christopher Pike. It's earned that slot."

—Justin Arnold, author of
Wicked Little Things and *Keep It In the Dark*

"Covered in green goo and nostalgia from beginning to end! *CodeSkull* by Chloe Spencer is the *Oregon Trail* x *Jumanji* x Goosebumps mashup former 90s kids and new YA horror fans alike are sure to love."

—Wendy Dalrymple, author of
Birthday Party Demon and *White Ibis*

"*CodeSkull* is the kind of book that feels like it was written for me. A 90s-set pixelated dread that creeps out of the virtual realm and exposes itself into our reality, where it becomes a breathing horror that's a fresh spin on the trope of a haunted videogame. It's the exact kind of thing you want from a story built on Fear Street vibes; our protagonists running around unsupervised, an older kid who's somewhat of a mentor, unconventional methods of fighting back against a supernatural threat, stakes that feel big but not silly. And it does all of that without ever losing sight of character. Spencer lets her characters be real kids, kids who have big, complicated feelings. You really can't ask for more."

—T.T. Madden, author of
Gorman's House and *The Familialists*

"Chloe Spencer can put heavy emotion into any story, *CodeSkull* is exhibit Z of this. Imagine Nick Arcade as a Saturday Morning Cartoon hosted by the Crypt Keeper and you've got *CodeSkull*!"

—Damien Casey, author of
Church of Skatan and *Shark-Squatch*

"Truly a fun, spooky time! If you loved *Goosebumps*, you'll love *Codeskull*."

—I.S. Belle, author of
Zombabe and the *Honeybloods* trilogy

"To destroy it, wouldn't you just ... break it?" Mick asked.

Cain shook his head, folding his arms against his chest. "No. That's not how this works. If you destroy the floppy disc, you unleash the demon, and he's free to possess something else."

"So when we played the game ... and didn't exit it without asking for permission ..."

His voice was rain against storm windows, soft yet threatening.

"You unleashed him."

Chloe Spencer

MADAXEMEDIA.COM

Published by Mad Axe Media

madaxemedia.com

The Totally Freaked! series is an original creation of Mad Axe Media.

Edited by Nico Bell

Book Cover & Interior Design by Joey Powell

Print ISBN: 978-1-966497-00-4

E-Book ISBN: 978-1-966497-01-1

To the boy I met in the 6th grade: Here's to us and all
our karaoke car trips.

Content Warning

CodeSkull includes blood, usage of knives, scary imagery, car crashes, on page deaths, injury, brief descriptions of dead bodies, and some strong/crude language. Please note that this is a work of fiction and the actions within this story should never be replicated at home.

Chapter One

Tanner pushed her horn-rimmed glasses up her sniffle-red nose. "If you don't like Tommy, why do you keep playing with him?"

On the arcade screen, Mick's character, Dig Dug, frantically scrambled away from the wide-eyed Fygar, which hissed and spat technicolor fire. Mick's fingers spammed the controls, performing an intricate dance away from the attacker, but as soon as she was about to escape, it hit her: the Pooka, which had flown to her character in a near-invisible haze, suddenly materialized right in her path. *WHOMP! Boooooo-ooh-whoop!* Her character collided with the Pooka, then crumpled to the ground in defeat. Mick clenched her teeth as she released a strangled scream of frustration.

That had been her last life.

With a heavy sigh, she looked at her score, blistering and red. 856,452. They had been there for several hours, trying to best her previous, and she had come only a few thousand from her goal. Grief bubbled up in Mick's chest like smoke in a chimney, but rather than cry, she ferociously punched in her initials: **M**ichelle **O**livia **D**aniels. Tanner sighed heavily, both annoyed by Mick's fury and her inability to respond to a basic question. Tanner stared down at her weathered tennis shoes and kicked away a dusty gumball which rolled underneath the adjacent arcade machine.

Mick turned back to Tanner, her arms folded across her chest. "Because he's an asshat, and I want him to suffer the taste of defeat, over and over again, until he stops saying crap like 'Girls can't play video games.'"

"I wouldn't give Tommy the time of day."

"Tanner, can I use your computer or not?"

A heavy sigh. "I guess."

"Awesome."

Mick reached into her backpack and touched the floppy disk that Tommy Perlaza had only given her hours ago this morning, after snidely wishing her luck on beating her previous score. She didn't know where Tommy got the idea that he could talk to her that way—after all, he hadn't even made it close in *Dig Dug*. The only reason Tommy thought he was so special was because he once made it to the 200th level of *Galaga*. Big whoop. *Galaga* sucked ass anyways.

"What even is that game?" Tanner asked as Mick zipped up her bag again.

"Tommy says it's a text-based RPG. Y'know, like *Rogue* or *Colossal Cave Adventure*."

Tanner made a face as she crouched down to pick up her backpack as well. "Those are *so* old, Mick."

"But they're classics."

"Whatever. I'd rather be playing *Mortal Kombat*."

"Yeah, so you can swoon over Liu Kang." Mick stuck out her tongue.

"Liu Kang is hella hot. It's not my fault you don't have good taste."

"I know, I know," Mick said, chuckling. She swung her backpack over her shoulder and picked up her empty soda, the fifth one that she had had today. "You tell me every chance you get."

Side by side, the girls wandered through the maze of arcade machines, careful to avoid bits of trampled gum and pieces of fossilized popcorn kernels from who-knows-when. Most of the newer games—the *Mortal Kombats*, the *Street Fighters*—were occupied by teenage boys who reeked of sweat and Funyons. Mick resisted the urge to shudder in horror when one kid licked the nacho grease off his hand and put it back on the joystick. The pinball machines, the noisiest and most vibrant space in Gearscore, were the stomping grounds for a lot of the older men in town. Mick passed by some of her classmates' dads, who were halfheartedly trying to hide the beer cans that they had snuck into the space by placing them underneath the machine. She smiled at them as they passed.

When they exited the brick-and-mortar building, they both hissed and recoiled from the light of the sun, like vampires, faux-clawing at the sky above in a desperate attempt to shield their eyes. Sometimes the rapid sun exposure genuinely hurt them, but they mostly liked freaking out the passerby. The more they put into their performance, the bigger the reaction. A teenage boy scrunched up his nose in disgust as he pushed past them, and the girls exchanged mischievous looks. The afternoon sun was a fried egg high in the sky, hot and wholesome. Mick tilted her head back, allowing the rays to wash over her like rain.

Mick and Tanner walked over to their bikes, still securely locked to the stands, and strapped on their helmets.

"Wow, the breeze out here feels nice today." Tanner stretched and smiled. The dandelion-yellow summer sun reflected on her cherub face, sure to sprinkle it with more freckles. "You know, maybe it would do us some good to go to a pool this summer or something. Catch a tan."

Mick made a face. "I don't tan. I burn."

Chapter Two

When her older brother Liam went to St. Olaf, Tanner moved into his former bedroom, which was in the attic. Earlier that summer, Mick and Tanner had plastered the space with posters and hung beaded rainbow curtains from the rafters which separated the "bedroom" from the "study," or the area that Tanner kept her books and the old Dell OptiPlex that her parents had gifted her so long ago, after they couldn't figure out how to use it. Although dated by 1998's standards, "Opti" was affectionately referred to as their mutual bestie. From Friday nights spent typing up stories in WordPerfect to exploring countless games, he was firmly a part of their life and friend group.

When Mick leaned over to put the floppy disk in the drive, she patted the monitor. "Good Opti."

"My computer isn't a dog."

Tanner retrieved a box of tissues from her nightstand and trotted over. She blew her nose three times, each sounded as stuffy as the last. Mick didn't pay any attention to her. Tanner grimaced as she sat down beside her friend. Outside, a thunderstorm rumbled, its energy rattling the windows.

"I hope we don't lose power," Tanner grumbled.

The computer clicked and whirred, attempting to load the game. Within a few moments, the program loaded. A string of glimmering lime green letters sashayed across the upper part of the screen:

CODESKULL

"I've never heard of this one," Tanner said as she chucked her used tissues in the waste bin. "Must be old. What's it about?"

"I don't know. Tommy didn't give me the box, only the case."

"Why did you take the game from him if you don't know what it's about? I mean, what if it's boring?"

Mick grinned. "What if it's not?" She cracked her knuckles, then her neck, before settling her hands on the keyboard, coated in its familiar stickiness—courtesy of a spilled soda can once or twice. "Tommy said it scores you based on how good your decisions are. Like, you make a smart choice, you get like 100 points. A bad one, you lose points. He wanted me to beat his score."

Tanner's eyes flitted over to the Kit-Cat Clock ticking on her wall, its tail sashaying from side to side. "What was his score?"

"Like 9000 or something."

"Are we going to be here all night?" Tanner squirmed in her seat. "I thought you and I were going to catch that showing of *Halloween H20* tonight."

"That's supposed to be a bad film anyways."

Tanner's bushy eyebrows set in a firm line. She scoffed and leaned back in her chair. Mick elbowed her.

"Hey. We'll check this game out, and if it sucks, we'll quit, okay?"

"Fine." The displeasure did not erode from Tanner's face.

Mick rubbed her hands together excitedly before she pressed the Enter key. On the screen, words materialized, and after a few seconds, formed a dense paragraph against the solid black background.

WELCOME TO CODESKULL. I AM PLEASED TO MEET YOU. ARE YOU READY TO BEGIN?

Mick took a deep breath before typing in her response: "Yes."

IF YOU ARE SO SURE, YOU'RE ABOUT TO EM-BARK ON A SPINE-TINGLING ADVENTURE UN-LIKE ANY OTHER. THROUGHOUT THE GAME, I WILL BE GRADING THE INTELLIGENCE OF YOUR CHOICES BASED ON HOW YOU RESPOND TO CERTAIN SITUATIONS. THE SMARTER YOUR DE-CISION, THE BETTER YOUR SCORE.

"How could it even make that determination?" Tanner muttered, unimpressed. "No code could possibly be sophisticated enough to do that."

"Do you not remember *System Shock?*" Mick asked.

Tanner shuddered, hugging her knees to her chest. "I try to forget, but SHODAN speaks to me in my nightmares. But *System Shock* came out in '94. I thought this game was like, way older than that?"

"Dude." Mick gripped the mouse a little too tightly. "Are you going to keep buggin', or are we going to play this game?"

"Continue, princess."

Mick glanced back at the screen. A new block of text appeared.

IT'S VERY IMPORTANT TO ASK MY PERMISSION

BEFORE EXITING THE GAME.
SO THAT I CAN SAVE YOUR PLACE.
DO YOU UNDERSTAND?

Mick responded: "Yes."

EXCELLENT. ALLOW ME TO SET THE SCENE.

A *whooshing* sound echoed from the speakers, and Mick couldn't tell if it was meant to mimic wind or water crashing over rocks close to shore. The screen remained black.

Tanner wrinkled her nose. "Did it break already?"

Mick clicked the mouse a few times, trying to get the game to respond.

PATIENCE. WE HAVE TO SET THE SCENE.

Mick's eyebrows rose. "Wicked."

YOU ARE A TRAVELER, BUT YOU ARE NOT ALONE. YOU HAVE A COMPANION WITH YOU. IS THIS COMPANION FRIEND OR FOE?

"Ooh. This is a cool choice," Mick said, her fingers grazing the keyboard. "What do you think, Tanner? You want to be the friend or the foe?"

"Friend," Tanner said.

Mick typed in the response.

FRIEND. NICE OF YOU TO HAVE A FRIEND TO ACCOMPANY YOU ON THIS OMINOUS NIGHT ... WHAT WITH THE RAIN POUNDING ON THE WINDOWS ...

Tanner pushed her glasses up her nose again and glanced to the window, which was streaked with rain drops. Somehow in their frustration to set up the game, they hadn't noticed that it finally started raining.

YOU AND YOUR COMPANION ARE WEARY, TRAVELER. YOU'VE BEEN WALKING THROUGH THE FOREST OF DARKNESS FOR SEVERAL

HOURS BY NOW. BUT AS YOU ROUND ANOTH-
ER WINDING CORNER, YOU COME ACROSS A
HOME.

Graphics emerged: a plethora of dark trees, pixelated and grainy, surrounded the edges of the screen. In the center, a small trail, trodden with digital kelly green grass, led a winding way to a buttercup yellow house. The image rested on the screen for so long that Mick pressed the Enter and arrow keys, trying to see if there was a way she could propel the character forward. After pressing the "up" arrow, her character emerged from the shadows of the trees, walking forward. The character had long brown hair and blue clothing. As she held down the arrow, another character materialized with cropped blond hair and pink clothing.

Tanner arched her brow. "I thought that this game was text-based?"

"I guess not?" Mick said. "I mean, I didn't get much of a chance to talk to Tommy before he told me he had to bounce."

"Why did he have to bounce?"

"Something about taking care of his little sisters or whatever."

Mick attempted to press the down arrow to see if her character would go backwards only to be met with a lecturing line from the game:

NOW NOW. I DIDN'T SAY YOU COULD TURN
BACK, DID I?
YOU STARTED IT. YOU FINISH IT.
UNLESS OF COURSE, YOU ASK FOR PERMIS-
SION TO SAVE YOUR PLACE.

Mick frowned. "Kinda weird."

"Really? You've played a lot more RPGs than me. I thought if your character wasn't supposed to go in a certain area, the game was supposed to tell you not to do that."

"Usually a game doesn't outright tell you that. It puts up a wall or an object in the pathway. I can't remember the last time a narrator would've said something to me." Mick scratched her head. "Maybe it's trying to—what would our English teacher call it? Break..."

"Mrs. Lewinksy would say it breaks the fourth wall?"

"Yeah. Maybe it's trying to do that?"

"Ooh," Tanner said, and for the first time since they had sat down to play, her eyes sparkled with excitement. "Kinda like in *Ferris Bueller*?"

"Yeah. That's kinda dope."

It wasn't completely unusual to Mick that a video game would try to throw a curveball or two like this. She remembered playing through *Castlevania: Symphony of the Night* on the PlayStation and how the castle had completely flipped upside down at a certain point, forcing her to replay the game. If anything, seeing how weird this was, it sunk in that this was going to be good.

And served as an annoying reminder that maybe Tommy Perlaza had good taste.

Glued to the edge of their seats, the girls leaned closer to the computer screen. Outside, rain continued to pitter-patter against the windows, its pace increasing.

Tanner looked outside and shuddered. "It's getting pretty bad. Are you going to be okay to ride your bike home later tonight?"

Mick didn't even acknowledge the question. Tanner realized her friend either didn't hear her or was *so* not concerned in that moment. Pressing the up key again, Mick guided her characters down the pathway. Pixelated and grainy trees fell to the wayside, and the house loomed bigger and bigger.

"The camera doesn't even cut away. It just zooms in," Mick said. "That's so cool."

Now that they were closer to the house, their characters had more details too. The brunette had small flecks of red across its chest, resembling a pattern. The other character, the blonde, had yellow stripes on is abdomen.

Tanner gasped. "*Dude.*"

"What?"

"Dude. That's *us.*"

Mick squinted at the characters, then at their own clothing. She was wearing a navy t-shirt with red cherries on it, courtesy of the last Old Navy summer blowout sale that her mom had bothered to attend. Tanner was wearing a pink shirt with yellow stripes. The characters' hairstyles were also similar to their own: Mick's with long, brown hair and Tanner's short and blond. It was uncanny, but then again, it was pixel art. How many different character designs could someone create with a limited palette and like, MS Paint? Or whatever the heck game designers used to make a game?

"Just coincidence," Mick decided.

"Coincidence? They've even got my glasses, dude. Look at those circles around blondie's eyes. What else could those be?"

Mick parsed through her mind for a logical explanation to this conundrum. Maybe there was some sort of character creator that they had bypassed? Maybe Tommy, who had last had the game, managed to create the characters and then save the game as soon as he'd done it? But then that begged the question, how did he know what they were going to wear that day? Did he see them earlier in town, go home to generate their characters, and then doubled back to the arcade to give Mick the game? The thought seemed ludicrous but plausible. The game had obviously creepy overtones, and knowing Tommy, he'd jump at the chance to freak them out.

Tanner's persnickety tone snapped Mick out of her train of thought. "What weirdness have you gotten us into?"

"Chillax, okay? I'm sure there's an explanation for this," Mick said. "Tommy's probably messing with us. Besides, you said that you'd give the game a fair shot."

Tanner's finger almost turned white when she pressed it hard against the screen. Her finger covered one of the windows of the yellow house that their characters were standing in front of. Something green and bulbous crept up one side of the house with faint flecks of white shining through.

"Do you see that?" Tanner said, her voice trembling. "That's—that's the trellis outside my old bedroom window. The bedroom I had before moving into the attic."

"What?" Mick squinted at the structure again. "No it's not."

"Mick," Tanner said, insistent. "That's the outside of my house."

"There's one, two, three... How many windows do you have on the outside of your house?"

"I don't know."

"Well, run out and check."

"In the rain?" Tanner cried out, cheeks red with fury. "Dude! Come on! That's so totally my house!"

"I don't see the attic window."

Mick rolled her mouse over the house in search of it but couldn't find anything. Even if this was a perfect recreation of Tanner's house—which Mick didn't think it was—she still thought it was possible that Tommy could be messing with them. But mostly, she wanted to get at least a little further in the game before turning it off. She wondered if Tanner was being extra dramatic so that she could pressure Mick into doing something else. Tanner did that sometimes, and it was *sooo* annoying. There was that one time in the third grade when Mick had wanted to go fairy hunting in the woods, but Tanner was so freaked out and insistent that kidnappers lived out there that Mick had given up before she even started. Mick was older now. She knew that fairies didn't exist, and that kidnappers probably didn't live in the woods.

And she *knew* that Tanner was too old to believe in any ridiculous things like that, too.

Mick pressed down on the arrow keys again, moving the characters closer to the house. Tanner gasped, shocked by Mick's carelessness. She attempted to reach forward and press the EXIT button, but Mick slapped her hand away from the keyboard. It didn't hurt, but the fact that Tanner would treat her so childishly really pissed her off.

"Dude!" she cried out, outraged. "Stop it!"

"Stop it?" Tanner repeated. "This is *my* computer."

"That's not fair! You said that I could play—"

"—You strongarmed me into it—"

"—because I want to play it, Tanner! *Jee-zus*!" Mick cried out. "It's a free video game, why wouldn't I want to play it?"

"If you want to play this creepy game so bad, why don't you go home and play it on your own computer? Oh, wait, I'm sorry, you don't have one! Which is *not* my problem!"

"Real mature, Tanner," Mick spat back, the words hot like venom against her tongue. "I don't know why you're being such a baby about this—"

"—Tan-tan, honey!" A honey-sweet voice echoed out from downstairs, interrupting them both.

Tanner took a deep breath before yelling back, "What do you want, Mom?!"

"Tanner!" Mrs. Reade replied, the honey burning now. "Get down here! I have to talk to you before we leave!"

With a huff, Tanner pushed back her chair and launched to her feet, stomping over to her door. She wrenched it open, nearly tearing through one of the posters she had tacked to it in the process. As she turned back to Mick, she pointed a stern finger at her.

"When I get back up here, this computer better be shut down. Do you understand me?"

Mick glared at her in response, saying nothing. Tanner rolled her eyes and stomped out of the room, then down the stairs. Tanner and her mother started talking about something, but Mick wasn't so much as enticed to eavesdrop. Of *course* Tanner would rub it in her face that she didn't have a computer. Typical Tanner. What was Mick supposed to say in response to that? *"Sorry I'm not a rich kid?" "Sorry my parents don't want me to have a computer?" "Sorry that I can't get a computer until I babysit those snot-nosed Rabblemacher kids from down the road a hundred times over?"* It wasn't fair. Tanner was lucky; she was the youngest in her family, so she got all the hand-me-downs from Liam. Mick was an only child, but unlike other only children whose parents spoiled them rotten, Mick's were too preoccupied with work—and money—to shower her with attention. The last time that they'd taken a family vacation, Mick was twelve years old, and it was to visit her Grandma Lucy up in Maine. *Maine.* Well, okay, Maine had been pretty cool and the seafood had been awesome, but that wasn't the point. Mick didn't have what Tanner had, and Tanner knew it.

So she didn't heed her friend's warning. She turned back to the game and led the characters right up to the front door of that eerie little house.

The game's narrator once again interrupted.

I FELT SOMEONE'S BODY HEAT LEAVE THE
ROOM.
I THOUGHT IT WAS YOURS.

Mick's eyes widened as she read the words.

REMEMBER. YOU HAVE TO ASK ME FOR PER-
MISSION TO SAVE THE GAME.
STEPPING AWAY FROM THE GAME AND LEAVING
THE COMPUTER ON DOESN'T COUNT.
DO YOU UNDERSTAND ME?
THIS IS YOUR LAST WARNING.

Mick swallowed a nervous lump in her throat as she typed, once again, "Yes."

GOOD. NOW... YOU AND YOUR COMPANION
HAVE ARRIVED AT A QUAINT LITTLE HOUSE. YOU
OPEN THE DOOR AND STEP INSIDE.

When Mick opened the door to the house, her jaw dropped.

Chapter Three

The first thing that caught Mick's eye were a series of pixels dividing the center of the screen in a cascade of fluorescent rainbow. Adjacent to that was a window, circular and small. Then came the pieces of furniture: bookshelves, a bed, a nightstand, a desk ...

Mick was staring at a perfect recreation of Tanner's bedroom.

Just as in real life, rain pounded against the window. Little pixel pellets pelted the frosted glass. Thunder built upon thunder as the sound from the computer combined with the noise outside, building to a near deafening crescendo. Jaw open, Mick watched as their characters shuffled into the room but took no further action. For several moments, it was a frozen screen and the sound of the rain in real life competing with the sound of the rain emanating from the computer monitor. Mick clicked the screen, panic bubbling in her throat, trying to figure out what was going on. *This can't be happening. This can't.* Even if Tommy had created their characters for them, there was no way he knew what the inside of Tanner's bedroom looked like. He had never been over to her house before.

"W-what's going on?"

Mick whipped around to see Tanner standing in the doorway, her eyes wide, jaw agape. She smashed both sides of her cheeks and shook her head over and over as she tiptoed closer to the computer.

"Oh my God," Tanner groaned. "I told you to turn this off!"

"Tanner," Mick cried out, reaching out for her. "Don't!"

But it was too late. Tanner ducked beneath the desk and yanked the computer's power cord out of the wall. The screen snapped from bright to black as a series of crackles and pops echoed through the air. The girls gasped, watching as green sparks erupted from the surface of the electrical outlet.

"Oh my God!" Tanner cried out. "What the hell is happening!?"

Springing to her feet, Mick yanked Tanner backwards, pulling her away from the effervescent green sparks. They littered the shag carpet like sprinkles on birthday cake before fizzling out of existence. Terrified, the girls clutched each other, fingers digging into their bare arms, their screams of terror trapped within their lungs. Eventually, the crackling stopped, but the girls remained frozen to their spots, transfixed.

"M-maybe it was the storm?" Mick suggested.

Tanner shook her head. Cautiously, she crouched down and approached the computer. With shaking hands, she picked up the power cord, and plugged it back in, then pressed the eject button on the desktop to eject the disc. Mick stared at her friend, watching as Tanner put the disc back in the plastic case, sealing it with an angry *CLICK*.

"I didn't save the game," Mick said, her voice hollow. "You shouldn't have done that."

"Michelle, you have to be kidding me!" Tanner snapped. "You're more concerned about saving the game than you are about why my room was in it!?"

"Don't call me Michelle!" She crossed her arms. "I'm concerned that we didn't follow the freaky game's instructions! It was very specific—"

"—Oh my God! Enough! Enough!" Tanner waved her hands wildly. "I wanted to go to the movies tonight, not play some creepy game that your *boyfriend* gave you—"

"—Tommy is not my boyfriend!" Mick snapped. "Why would you say that? That's not funny!"

"You know what's not funny? The fact that I asked you to shut down the game and you kept playing it." Tanner shuddered, rubbing the goosebumps that had erupted along her arms. She blinked repeatedly, as if trying to hold back tears, although Mick didn't see any. "It was totally being weird, and you wouldn't listen to me."

"Maybe because Tommy built it or something. I don't know!"

"Tommy could *barely* pass geometry, Mick! You think he knows how to make an entire video game by himself?" Tanner scoffed. "Besides that, I can't believe we did what you wanted to do the whole day, and that wasn't enough for you."

Mick stared at her, flabbergasted. "What do you mean? You said that you wanted to go to the arcade."

"Right, because I know you like the arcade. But it's not fun for me to sit and watch you game for like, four hours while I do nothing."

"You don't have to stand there and do nothing. You could've played something. I wouldn't have minded."

Tanner groaned, rolling her eyes. "Do you ever think about anyone other than yourself? That's not what I'm trying to say. I'm trying to say that I had *one* thing, *one* thing that I wanted to do tonight, and you straight up refused to do it. Because you'd rather do whatever Tommy wants you to do."

Mick stared at her friend. Words tumbled within her brain like wet clothing in a dryer, but she couldn't conjure anything useful to say. Part of her was frustrated that Tanner was pitching a fit about spending the day at the arcade when she hadn't said that she didn't want to. Even worse, she said that Mick only wanted to do things that Tommy Perlaza wanted her to do, which was *not* true. It was irritating that Mick was the one who almost always came up with their plans, and that Tanner didn't offer her input. Then again, when Tanner *had* made a suggestion about what they should do, Mick had shut her down. The miscommunication issues felt like a failure on both their parts, but the guilt was enough to make Mick's stomach gurgle with nausea. Normally, when they got into fights, Mick would be able to nod and sort of take it, but today, she felt the anger sting her tongue.

"Maybe if you didn't act like such a baby and used your words, we could've gone and done something else today," Mick said, her voice slow.

Tanner's eyebrows lifted. "Are you serious?"

"Are *you?* I don't sit there like a martyr and not say how I feel," Mick said. "You should try it sometime, instead of waiting until the last possible minute, when I really want to do something. And accusing me of being into Tommy is really gross on your part, considering everything that happened last year in middle school."

"Whatever."

"No, not whatever. How come you get to hit low, but I can't do the same?"

"It's not about hitting low! God, how are you the one calling me a baby when you're acting so childish?" Tanner pinched the bridge of her nose. "I think you should go home."

"It's still raining outside."

Tanner shook her head. "That's sort of not my problem, Mick." She slapped the floppy disc case into Mick's open hand. "Take your cursed crap game and get out of my house."

Their tension was interrupted by a symphony of bees. Startled, the girls turned towards the computer once more, as the buzzing grew louder, echoing from the speakers. An odd symbol burned across Opti's screen, continuing to materialize pixel by pixel until an object formed across the flickering screen.

A human skull. A three-dimensional, perfectly formed human skull. Pixels dripped down the screen, obscuring the eyeholes, smearing the slack open jaw. It melted down the screen, flooding into a pool of green. As the image continued to crumble, the buzzing noises reached their peak, drowning out the sounds of the storm. Mick covered her throbbing ears, grimacing. Tanner scrambled back to the computer and yanked out the power cord again. This time, no sparks popped out of the wall.

"Great," Tanner said, her voice trembling. "Now I've probably got a virus. My dad is *so* going to lose it."

Chapter Four

Tanner couldn't remember the last time she had spent a Friday night at home by herself, but maybe that was a good thing. After kicking Mick out of the house—who hadn't so much as offered an apology, thank you very much—Tanner retreated to her room and threw a spare blanket over her computer. Chills prickled the hairs of her arms. She knew it was childish, but if that random skull image was going to reappear, she was gonna lose it. With her parents out for their date night, she'd be alone for a while, and the last thing she wanted to do was call them crying and begging them to come home. They'd treated her like such a baby in the past, never allowing her to stay home by herself, but since Liam left, her parents had finally started to trust leaving her home unsupervised. Mick was a latchkey kid, and her parents had been leaving her alone since she was like, ten. This fall, she'd be starting high school. It felt ridiculous that her folks had waited this long to give her some level of independence.

And she would do nothing, absolutely *nothing*, to jeopardize that.

Outside, the thunderstorm rumbled: a growling dog on the verge of biting. At this point in the evening, Tanner wanted nothing more than to bite into dinner. Her mom had given her money for her and Mick to order pizza, but with Mick having left, Tanner decided that she'd rather pocket the cash to use at a later time, and dig into one of the Kid Cuisines her mom had stowed away in the freezer. Tanner could never say no to chicken nuggets, and that gooey chocolatey brownie that always scorched her tongue on the first bite but tasted so good.

Trotting downstairs, Tanner ruminated on what she wanted to do tonight. She had picked up a couple R.L. Stine volumes from the library the other day, so she could start one of those, or there might be something on Cartoon Network to watch, like *Animaniacs*. Heck, she'd even settle for an episode of *Ed, Edd n' Eddy*. Anything to distract her from the fight she had with Mick. They rarely fought—at best, they'd have playful arguments on which game was the best or which *Goosebumps* book was scariest—but the older they got, the more common these spats were. Worry was an ocean that flooded Tanner's brain and threatened to spill over from her now-stinging eyes. Was it possible that they were outgrowing this friendship? The two of them had been friends since Tanner had moved to town in the second grade. A friendship breakup was unfathomable to her, but perhaps it was inevitable. Her mom had often warned her of the changes that girls would go through as they grew up. For a long time, Tanner thought it was about puberty: growing hair in strange places and smelling like moldy cottage cheese if she went too long in between showers. Now, part of her wondered if her mom had meant the changes in friendships and personality types as well.

As she picked up the TV remote from the top of the TV, Tanner shook the upsetting thoughts from her brain. She pressed a button on the remote to turn it on and yelped as fire ants bit the tips of her fingers. The remote collided with the coffee table, the back of it popping off, and the batteries rolling onto the floor. Green sparks licked the edge of the device. Bewildered, Tanner staggered backwards. *Was everything on the fritz because of the storm?* She sucked on her wounded fingertips, still hot to the touch, as she moved from the living room and into the kitchen. *Hopefully I can still make my Kid Cuisine.*

Tanner crouched down in front of the fridge and pulled out the freezer drawer. Her wounded hand grazed past numerous freezer-burnt boxes and plastic bags full of years-old venison that her dad swore he was going to throw on the smoker one day before she finally snagged her precious box. As her hand closed around it, a sharp cold nipped at her fingers. Clouds of misty chill surrounded her, rising from the drawer and falling onto the floor in a blanket of fog. She retracted her hand, then slammed the freezer door shut, shaking her head. She cracked open the box, peeled back the layer of plastic, and popped it into the microwave sitting on the kitchen counter. After punching in the numbers, she pressed the start button.

But the microwave didn't go. Didn't so much as light up or start turning. Frowning, Tanner smacked it with the heel of her hand. It was an old one, its white surface yellowed from age, so it didn't surprise her that it was giving her issues. But smacking it didn't help, either. With a sigh, Tanner yanked the cord from the wall and plugged it back in before punching in the numbers once more. Still nothing.

"What the heck!" she cried out.

Tanner squinted at the tiny screen that the green numbers appeared on, trying to see if there was some sort of error message or some obvious step that she was missing. She realized that she wasn't looking at numbers, but a coagulation of pixels. Her heart caught in her lungs when she realized what it was.

A skull.

A tiny, misshapen skull.

With a shriek, Tanner scrambled backwards from the microwave as sparks began to buzz and crackle. In an instant, the yellow-orange light of the kitchen turned a nauseating shade of electric green, its saturated light casting deep shadows around the room. Clouds of cold air seeped through the cracks of the fridge door, obscuring Tanner's vision. She stumbled backwards, tripping over herself, and cried out in pain as her body collided with the corner of the kitchen table. Wheezing, she fell to the floor. Everything that had been stacked on the table's surface—papers, a stapler, and torn envelopes—pelted her head. Green fire erupted from every electrical surface: shooting up from the burners on the stove, blasting from the garbage disposal, and raining down from the light fixtures above. Sound erupted from everywhere, engulfing her ears in a tumultuous tornado of noise. The TV in the living room was on full blast, and every phone in the house rang simultaneously. Her mom's blender on the counter whirred to life, its spinning blades glinting in the green.

Tanner screamed as the electrical sparks from the light fixture above her burrowed into her skin. She watched as they sizzled and popped, her ivory skin burning like a marshmallow in campfire heat. Sobbing, she scrambled out of the way of the light fixture, right towards the blender that anxiously roared and waited for her.

When she was a child, Tanner's mom had often lectured her about her clumsiness. After all these years of playing video games with Mick, Tanner thought that her hand-eye coordination had at least improved some. But as her hand touched the surface of the blender's control panel, glowing green with an unfathomable evil, she realized that wasn't the case.

Unfortunately, she realized it too late.

Chapter Five

"Mickey?"

Mick peeled her head off of her pillow, eyes crusty with sleep. Even in the dead of summer, her bed was a warm cocoon from which she wanted no escape. Beside her on the pillow, her Gameboy Color lay, its screen black. As she rubbed her tired eyes, she wondered if she had bothered to save last night before the battery had died. She definitely did *not* want to replay the psychic gym in *Pokemon Blue.*

"Mickey?" Mick recognized her mother's voice on the other side, but it was different, fraught with tears. As she heard her mom choke back a sob, her eyes widened and she sprung to her feet, scrambling over to the door and ripping it open.

"Mom?" Mick cried out. "What's wrong?"

Mick stared into her mother's face, red and blotchy with tears. Her mom's hand clenched around the cordless phone that was usually in the kitchen downstairs. Whatever it was, her mom thought it was so important that she had to come upstairs and stir her from her slumber, which meant that it couldn't be good.

"Come here, sweet girl," her mom whispered, opening her arms wide for a hug. "Come here."

For a moment Mick stared at her mother, wary. Her parents were not touchy-feely people. They were hug-on-a-birthday kind of people, and the hug would be one of those awkward one-armed side embraces if anything. Truth be told, they were the last people that Mick would go to for any form of physical comfort. But at the urging of her tearful mother, Mick obliged, scooting closer. As her mother embraced her, she felt tears dampen the shoulder of her nightshirt and she resisted the urge to wriggle away. Her discomfort was not as all-consuming as the panic that had invaded her body. No matter how many deep breaths she took, nothing could have prepared her for the unbelievable thing her mother said next.

Mick left her house in a blur of tears and screams and shakes. Before she knew it, she had thrown on her sneakers and hopped on her bike. Still in her pajamas, she pedaled two streets over to where Tanner's house sat on the corner of Marsh and 5th. Her house, so familiar, so quaint, had now dissolved into chaos. An arsenal of police cars formed a blockade in the front yard, their tires slick with mud, and a fire truck sat in the driveway where Mr. Reade's Suburban usually rested. Lines of yellow tape criss-crossed their way across the yard and house. Neighbors stood at the end of the driveway, wrapped up in ragged robes, some of the moms with rollers in their hair from the night before. They embraced and sobbed, wiping tears from their eyes.

Mick didn't even bother to brake before leaping off her bike. It clattered to the asphalt ground, wheels spinning in a frenzy.

"Tanner!" Mick screamed. "Tanner!"

People came to her in droves, attempting to wrap their arms around her. They knew her, of course they knew her. She had been coming here almost every day since she was seven years old. She had memorized what they kept in their bathroom cabinets, what artwork hung on the wall in her father's study, and had committed the musk of Liam's bedroom, courtesy of Axe body spray, to memory. She wrestled and wriggled against them, fighting back all the bodies that had suddenly surrounded her with their warmth. Although their voices were sweet, their tones even, she couldn't help but be reminded of getting surrounded by zombies in *Resident Evil*. This was a horror game. She was stuck in a horror game, right? That had to be the only explanation.

Tanner couldn't be—

Tanner wasn't—

"Michelle." She heard Mrs. Reade call out over the din of the crowd. "You shouldn't be here."

"This—she's not—she can't be ..." Mick gasped, choking on her words. Tears flooded her eyes once more, obscuring her vision, and she collapsed to the ground.

"Michelle, honey," Mrs. Reade said, crouching down beside her.

Mrs. Reade's eyes—Tanner's eyes—were a muddled watercolor of tears and smudged makeup. She sobbed, the kind of sob that grownups only make when they had been completely deprived of hope. Mick hadn't heard someone sob like that since Grandma Lucy had died. And that was when she knew that it was real.

Tanner was gone.

And in that moment, she finally allowed herself to be embraced.

freak electrical accident. That was the most Mrs.
Reade was willing to tell her, although Mick
suspected that the real gruesome details were deliber-
ately left out. She had heard some of the neighbors
muttering about being "burnt to a crisp" and "the body
was unrecognizable." The fire department's explanation was that Tanner had turned on too many electrical
appliances all at once, which caused an outlet to surge,
and burst into flames. The firefighters suspected it was
a result of last night's thunderstorm, that perhaps the
electrical system was unstable. Tanner's death had sent
the neighborhood into a panic. That morning, before
Mick's parents had swung by to pick her up, she had

watched a few neighbors haul armfuls of electronics out to their trash cans and dumpsters, chucking them away. Their metal glinted in the overcast sunlight, twinkling like stardust. The bewildered firefighters scratched their heads, seemingly at a loss for how this catastrophe had possibly transpired.

Well, Mick had a hunch.

After she returned home, her parents urged her to go back to bed. They closed her blinds and turned on her fan and shut her away. Maybe they thought they were helping, but Mick felt like they were doing what they always did: push her emotions out of sight and out of mind. She cried, yes, but she knew she couldn't sit there and cry this whole time. Something had happened last night when they were playing CodeSkull; something had been unleashed, and it had invaded the electrical wires of the Reade family's home. It wasn't a logical explanation, but Tanner's death defied the rules of logic.

Yet even knowing that, she couldn't bring herself to leave her bed. Grief was a thorned and wild vine that twisted up the wall of tragedy. Tanner, *her* Tanner, was gone? Tanner, who had always gifted her one Cosmic Brownie for each year she was alive on her birthdays? Tanner, her faithful player two in every disastrous round of *Ice Climbers* she had ever played? Tanner, who knew Mick better than she knew herself?

How could she be gone?

Minutes drifted into hours. Mick's entire world shrunk to the darkness beneath the quilt her grandmother had sewn for her. That is, until her mother knocked on her door again.

"Baby?" Her mother warbled. "Someone's here to see you."

Bleary-eyed, Mick raised her head from her pillow. Her voice was cracked asphalt as she spoke. "I don't want to see anyone."

"I know, sweetheart, but I don't think it'll take long. He said he's trying to get his game back. Did you borrow a game from him?"

At once, Mick's eyes flashed open, and her nerves electrified, humming with righteous fury.

Tommy.

Tommy had come to see her.

In an instant, Mick sat up. "Send him in."

Her mom's grip tightened on the door. "You're sure you have the game?"

"Yep." Mick clenched her fists under the covers. *A game of knuckle sandwich.* "Send him in."

Nodding, her mom walked away, presumably back to the front door where Tommy waited. Mick glanced at the game, which was sitting in its case on her nightstand. Her heartbeat thrummed with a mixture of anxiety and anger, and she grabbed the case, clenching it so tightly in her hands that her knuckles blanched white.

Tommy stepped into her doorway. He was a bit on the rounder side and still short—he hadn't yet hit his growth spurt that most boys their age were promised. A part of Mick suspected that he never would. His brown eyes, as wide as oceans, were surrounded by beaches of freckles, mahogany brown against his tawny skin. Some of his curls flopped down in front of his forehead, which was plastered with sweat. Mick's mother murmured something before drifting away to attend to something else, and in the moments of silence that followed, it took all of Mick's strength to not leap from her bed and pound the living daylights out of him.

"I—I heard from Maggie this morning," he rasped. He sounded out of breath, like he had run all the way here. Tommy was one of the few kids in their grade that didn't even have a scooter to get around town with. "Who heard it from Linda, who heard it from Chelsea, and—Mick, I am so, so sorry."

Mick stared at Tommy as rage boiled in her belly like a pot of water left to boil on the burner. Yet at the sound of his voice, so soft and genuine, she felt her fists relax, her fingers uncurl. She swallowed a lump in her throat.

"What have you done?" she asked him.

Tommy's eyes narrowed in confusion. "What ... what do you mean?"

"The game," Mick snapped. "Do you know what happened in that game?"

"The game?" he asked her. "W-What do you mean?"

"*This*. Codeskull," she hissed, slapping the case down on the bed so hard. "This stupid game that you gave us had some weird stuff going on, Tommy. Where the hell did you get it from?"

"Weird stuff? What do you mean, weird stuff?"

"It knew where we lived."

"W-what do you mean, it knew where you lived?"

Mick launched into her explanation of yesterday's events: how the game had perfectly recreated her and Tanner in pixel form, how it also seemed to have copied Tanner's house, and how the game's narrator had "spoken" to them. She also brought up how Tanner had unplugged the computer before she had a chance to save the game.

"It caused this weird electrical ... spark thing," Mick said. "The outlet almost exploded. It was the freakiest shit I have ever seen."

Tommy frowned. He wiped at the sweat on his forehead with the back of his hand and muttered something under his breath. Mick set her jaw.

"I'm sorry, *what* was that?" Mick asked, cupping a hand over her ear. "You know, you've got some nerve showing up here and then not offering so much as an explanation."

"I don't know *what* it was," Tommy said.

"What do you mean?"

"I've never played the game," he said.

Mick stared at him, her eyes bugging out of her head. Her heart lurched in her chest as though it had been thrown through the windshield of a car going 55 miles per hour. She clutched it, her voice rasping in her throat, her tone sinking as low as a grave. "What do you mean you never played the game?"

"I just—I didn't!" he sputtered. "When I went to Flicks Forever yesterday, the cashier tried to prevent me from checking it out. I just thought it was a super scary game or maybe it was rated M for mature and that's why he wouldn't let me have it."

"But you told me how it worked. You told me that it graded you based on how good your decisions were. Was that all a lie?"

"The score was a lie," Tommy said, "But not the rules. I overheard the cashier talking about it with another customer. I think it was the guy who last played the game or something."

Mick ran her tongue over her teeth. "Wait, so if the cashier wouldn't let you have it, how did you get it?"

"Well, I ..." Tommy's cheeks darkened. "I sorta... took it."

"You stole it?"

Tommy paused. Then he said, "I mean, if that's the wording that you want to use ..." He scratched the back of his head. "I needed to return my little sisters' movies today, but if he's there, I can't walk back in there without giving him that game back. Otherwise, I might get my ass beat."

After a momentous pause, Mick sighed, pinching the bridge of her nose. "Tommy Perlaza, you might be the dumbest piece of shit on the planet."

Chapter Seven

Mick's parents didn't ask too many questions when twenty minutes later, her and Tommy were out the door and on the sidewalk. For a brief moment she thought that they would care more, maybe prevent her from leaving, but her mom had simply nodded and told her that it'd be good to get some sunlight. Flicks Forever, Wildwood's only video rental store, was about half an hour from her house. She would've been on her bike, but since Tommy didn't have one, she had no choice but to plod along the cracked cement sidewalks, the heat of the summer sun beating down on her. At least this time she remembered to wear her baseball cap—a ratty Twins one Gramps had bought for her when she was five. She didn't really like baseball, or sports of any kind for that matter, but she loved that hat.

Tommy wiped more sweat from his forehead. "I still don't understand what you think Tanner's death has to do with the game."

"Because of the electricity," she said. "Am I supposed to believe it's just all coincidence? As if."

"I mean, maybe? What if there was something seriously wrong with the Reades' house? How do you know the firefighters are making things up?"

"I spent *years* of my life in that house, Tommy. There's nothing unsafe about it," Mick snapped. "And it's not like Tanner could've done anything to an appliance to cause it to overload and burst into flames or something. That just doesn't happen. I owe it to Tanner to figure this out. She was my only friend." She swallowed a lump in her throat, though thankfully, no tears rose to her eyes. She'd rather walk out into traffic than cry in front of Tommy Perlaza.

Tommy glanced at her. "She wasn't your only friend."

"No, Tommy, she was."

"But I thought that you had more friends than that. What about Louise? And Peggy?"

Mick stopped dead in her tracks, shooting him a death glare. "Are you kidding me?"

"What?"

"You *know* what happened in middle school. Don't play dumb." She tossed her head, brown strands falling in front of her face. "I've had enough of you doing that."

"I'm not! I seriously don't know what happened!" Tommy snapped. "And would you quit calling me stupid? I'm not the one who struggled to get a passing grade in English last year. It's not even my first language."

Mick's cheeks burned. "Maybe if we hadn't been forced to read the most boring book in the world—"

"—*The Great Gatsby* is one of the most popular books in history—"

"—and it sucks, Tommy. It sucks eggs," Mick snapped. "And if you're going to rag on my grades in English, then maybe we should talk about how you have had to do every extra credit worksheet in math class since the fifth grade."

"Math is *way* harder than English, and my grades are better than yours, stupid!"

"Now who's calling who stupid?"

"You know what? Maybe if you weren't such a total bitch, you'd have more friends, Mick!"

They stared at each other, chests as puffed as proud peacocks. They were on the edge of an intersection, and cars zoomed by them in a cloud of exhaust and shiny-sparkly metal. They were getting closer and closer to downtown Wildwood.

Tommy deflated first. "I'm sorry. I didn't mean to call you a bitch."

"Yes, you did."

"Yes, I did, but maybe you deserved it." Tommy grinded his teeth as he pressed the walk button to cross the intersection. His voice remained strained yet soft as he spoke. "I know that you're hurting, Mick. And I'll try to help you get some answers, as long as you try your best to get along with me. Deal?"

He stretched his hand out to her. Mick stared at it for the briefest of moments, then slapped her palm against his. Their handshake was firm—a binding contract. Then Mick gagged and wiped her hand on the leg of her bermuda shorts.

"Why are you so sweaty?"

"In case you haven't noticed, it's 86 degrees out-side, and there's humidity." Tommy wiped his forehead again. His curls had gone flat, plastered against his head in a sheen of black. "Let's hope that the AC is working in that stupid video store."

Although Flicks Forever had been a longstanding in-stitution in Wildwood, that did not mean it was par-ticularly beloved. Stepping in through the front doors, the stench of mildew was almost unbearable. The two times Mick had been in here within the past year, she had watched the owner scrub at a mold stain on one of the ceiling tiles. Every so often they'd haul out their moldiest VHS tapes and sell them on discount. Tanner had got her copy of *You've Got Mail* from here and promptly threw out the box as soon as she had forked over the two dollars and fifty cents it had cost.

Mick wiped at her eyes. *Tanner.* She couldn't think about her right now. She had to put her game face on, at least until she got some answers. Fortunately for Mick, she wouldn't have to wait long, for no more than five seconds after the little bell had rung, the cashier had leapt over the counter.

"You!" he snarled, pointing an accusatory finger—speckled with black and white nail polish—in Tommy's direction. "You're going to give me that game back or I'm going to rip your throat out, you little shit!"

Mick and Tommy stood there, frozen, as the cashier reached into the pocket of his black leather pants and whipped out a switchblade. Tommy shrieked. An actual, honest-to-goodness high-pitched shriek. What happened next blew by in a flash: Tommy scrambling down one aisle, the teenage cashier chasing right after him. Flabbergasted, Mick stood there, unsure of how to intervene. She may have won several rounds of *Street Fighter* and *Mortal Kombat*, but when faced with a real weapon, she had no desire to test her luck in real life. As Tommy toppled one shelf of VHS tapes, crashing to the floor, Mick finally sprung into action, chasing after the knife-wielding cashier. She darted around the corner and latched onto his arm with the strength of a spider monkey.

"Hey, hey, hey!" Mick cried. "Chillax! We brought it back!"

The cashier whipped around to face her, his lips curled back in a snarl. Up close, Mick could make out all the intricate details of his face. High cheekbones, broad nose, thick lips painted black, stark against the earthy mahogany of his skin. Short black locs drifted in front of his face. Multiple piercings lined the edges of his ears, some studs, some rings, all of them sparkly and silver. Mick had seen and heard about him before, but she couldn't remember his name. Though she parted her lips to speak, no sound would come out. He scoffed, sheathing his knife and sliding it into his pocket once more.

"Not like it matters," he said. "Now that someone's dead."

Grief and fear washed over Mick. "What do you mean?"

"I mean," the boy said, gesturing to Tommy, "he got a little girl killed last night."

"A little girl?" Mick's eyes narrowed. "Do you mean Tanner Reade?"

"I don't know her name," he spat back. "I only know what *this* asshat did. Stealing from me? You must be out of your damn mind, thinking you can walk back in here and not get your ass beat."

"Hey," Mick said, trying to get his attention again. The boy's shoulders bristled, but there was something surfacing in his brown eyes—something as soft as sadness. The anger was not borne from bloodlust, but grief. "If you're talking about the girl that died last night, her name was Tanner Reade, and she was my best friend. The one who got electrocuted by all of her kitchen appliances. I'm Mick Daniels, and this is Tommy Perlaza."

Some emotion flickered in the boy's eyes, but he didn't say anything. He stood there, stiffly. Tommy peeled himself off of the tile floor, rubbing a blackened bruise that had appeared on his knee. He staggered to his feet as Mick reached into her backpack and pulled out the disc. The boy snatched it back from her and examined it in his hands. Now that they were standing still, she noticed his nametag: Cain Williams. A memory flickered like a flame in her mind.

"Cain," Mick said with a snap of her fingers. "You performed at the bandshell for the town's Fourth of July talent show last year, right? You played the bass."

Cain nodded, although his expression remained stoic. "I played the bass for one number, then keyboard the next."

"Right, right," Mick said. "I thought your band did an awesome job. I don't know much about punk, but I do listen to Bikini Kill sometimes, and I thought your energy was killer."

"Yeah," Tommy added, creeping back over to them. His eyes remained wild with fear as he spoke. "Y-you were really great."

"Can it," Cain spat at Tommy, then to Mick, "What happened? How did your friend get the game from this bozo?"

For the second time that day, Mick launched into her explanation of yesterday's events: on their way to the arcade, Tommy had run into them and given her and Tanner the game, then challenged them to beat his score. As time ticked by, Cain's eyes grew wearier, his posture deflating. By the time that Mick got to the end of her story, he had buried his face in his hands.

"No one was supposed to play it," Cain whispered. "No one was supposed to get hurt."

Canned laughter from some studio sitcom played on the TV nearest to them. Cain wiped at his eyes, shaking his head. Mick tilted her head in confusion.

"No one was supposed to play it? Then why was it at the store?"

"It wasn't like it was on sale or anything." Cain tapped the case's smooth surface. "See this? No barcode sticker to scan. The game wasn't for sale. It was sitting on the counter after a friend had dropped it off, and Tommy decided to run away with it."

"Your friend gave it to you?"

"Yes," Cain said, the words hot like sparks on his tongue. "To destroy. *Not* to play. I told Tommy to put it down and he didn't listen."

"It looked cool!" Tommy snapped. "I thought you were being a dick!"

"I was, but that clearly didn't stop you," Cain shot back.

"To destroy?" Confused, Mick waved her hands in a vague attempt to beg for clarity. "I don't understand. You were supposed to destroy it?"

"Yes, because as I'm sure you've found out, it's cursed. I learned about it in chat rooms on AIM."

"Chatrooms?" For all her years of computer gaming, Mick had barely spent any time on the Internet, so while she'd heard of the term, she was unfamiliar with it. At Tanner's house, the dial-up was so slow that even when Mrs. Reade wasn't on the phone yapping to her friends and some sixth cousin twice removed in Utah, there was no point in them trying to use it. Plus, they both hated the sounds that the modem made.

"There're chat rooms for everything you can think of," Cain said. "And I like learning about the occult, so I was in a few servers. My friend found it at some kind of pawn shop, and he didn't know how to destroy it, so he brought it to me."

"To destroy it, wouldn't you just ... break it?" Mick asked.

Cain shook his head, folding his arms against his chest. "No. That's not how this works. If you destroy the floppy disc, you unleash the demon, and he's free to possess something else. My plan was to perform a ritual that would safely destroy the floppy disc with the demon inside it."

"So ..." Mick swallowed. "So when we played the game ... and didn't exit it without asking for permission ..."

His voice was rain against storm windows, soft yet threatening. "You unleashed him."

Chapter Eight

A heavy weight settled within Mick's chest. *You unleashed him.* How had this situation unfolded? How could Tommy's decision to do a harmless prank lead to Tanner's death? And what exactly did "unleashing" this creature entail? Goosebumps prickled her arms, and her body stiffened as though rigor mortis had set in. Once again, she tried to speak, but words wouldn't form on her lips.

Cain crouched to the floor and began to pick up some of the VHS tapes that Tommy had knocked over. After a brief pause, Tommy and Mick both came to his aid, picking up a few and trying to make the dusty shelves look nice.

"What are we supposed to do now?" Mick whispered. "If we unleashed him, do you think he's gone?"

"We can hope." Cain rubbed his kohl-smudged eyes. "I don't know, though. We're not gonna know until another body shows up."

"I don't understand. Why would it ..." Mick swallowed. "Why would he kill Tanner?"

"Because he's a demon. CodeSkull is a demon," he said.

"It's name is CodeSkull? But the game is called CodeSkull," Mick said.

"Well, not like we can actually ask him what his name is," Cain replied. "Anyways, demons feed on chaotic energy. Killing things, torturing them—it makes them stronger."

Tommy's shoulders stiffened. "So if killing things makes him stronger, what reason does he have to leave town? Why wouldn't he keep killing?"

Keep killing? Keep killing? Keep killing? Mick twisted her pinkie in her ears, as if that would remove the echo of Tommy's voice. A gasp escaped Cain's lips. Slowly, Mick tilted back her head. TVs twisted outwards from each corner of the store and even from some beams. On each screen, she saw their three solemn little faces staring back at them.

"Why is the TV broadcasting security cam footage?" Mick whispered.

Her voice echoed around them as the screens of the TVs glitched purple and red, flickering rapidly. She watched as their facial features distorted, as Cain's eyes twisted into black holes, as her brown hair dripped down her body like globs of mud. Then green—pixels and pixels of shimmering green—leaked down the screen, obscuring their image. Slowly, the image of a skull superimposed over the chaos.

Cain grabbed both of their wrists. "We gotta bounce."

Green exploded around them like fireworks. The TV closest to them overloaded, lightning crackling from its pores and vents, striking the walls and tops of the displays closest to them. Immediately, the shelves ignited, filling their nostrils with the stench of smoldering plastic. Screaming, Tommy scrambled backwards, as another TV short circuited.

"Tommy, watch out!" Mick screamed, scrambling forward.

She tackled him, flattening him to the ground, out of harm's way. The sparks that would have otherwise exploded on his skin had now transformed into flames, gnawing through another display shelf full of Don Bluth movies. She rolled off of him, scrambling to her feet. Looking across the aisles, she saw Cain on the other side of the store, hustling towards the exit. As he sprinted past a TV, he grinned at the thrill of reaching the exit, but then a light overhead shattered, embers raining down. Cain yelped, crashing into a wall, only for another sconce above him to explode. He furiously patted his hair, trying to extinguish any sparks that had latched on.

Around them, the haze of smoke darkened. The remaining TVs, each with a skull still emblazoned across their screen, flickered through the increasing, noxious darkness. Mick yanked Tommy to his feet, ushering him towards the exit as fast as she could. More explosions. Shattered glass struck her like cat scratches, swift and stinging. Coughing, Mick pulled the collar of her shirt over her nose, trying her best to breathe. Cain held open the door for them as they scrambled through to the other side, away from the fire.

Now outside, the shrieks of the fire alarms rattled in her ears, rendering them raw. Mick plugged one of them with her fingers, turning back to look at the fiery monster that had swallowed the store whole. Even through the tinted windows, the green flames were visible; a thousand handprints pushed against the glass from the inside, demanding to be released.

"So that's his power," Cain said, grimacing.

"What?" Mick asked, turning in his direction. She watched as he continued to pat out a few sparks in his hair. "What do you mean, his power?"

"He travels through electricity, and can possess electrical objects," Cain said. "When you played the game, you unleashed him into the electrical wires of the Reade's house."

Tommy shook his head. "But how did he get here?"

"Everything in this town is connected to the same power plant," Cain said. "You didn't know that?"

Tommy snorted. "I know that. But electricity doesn't travel that fast, does it? H-He—*CodeSkull*—came from the other side of town. It's like we're dealing with the speed of light or whatever."

"Electricity travels at 1/100th the speed of light, so yeah, he can actually travel that fast," Cain replied, his eyes narrowing. He looked at Mick. "Is he tripping?"

"I've been asking myself that question every day since the fifth grade, Cain."

A crack of thunder split the sky above—or no, wait, that was the powerline overhead shorting out. Electrical sparks and fire rained down from above, and the cables snapped off one by one as the fire gnawed through it. Shrieking, the kids scrambled out of the way. Cain reached into the pocket of his pants and removed a set of keys, then gestured to a teal '92 Ford Taurus sitting at the back of the parking lot. He didn't need to say a word, not that he could have, he was running so hard.

As Cain unlocked the door, Mick and Tommy scrambled into the backseat, squashing forgotten Arby's wrappers and last year's half-finished homework. Cain climbed into the front seat and turned the key in the ignition. It sputtered and coughed.

"You piece of shit!" Cain yelled, then he licked his lips, his voice softening. He patted the dashboard like it was a horse he had to coax around a mountain path. "Come on, baby, come on ..."

Holding her breath, Mick turned to look out the rearview window. She gasped, watching as the surrounding power lines burst into flames. The first one that had gone up was now a forgotten candle on a toddler's cake—a smoldering mess that invaded the patches of dry grass below. Streetlights in the parking lot shattered, inching ever closer. *POP, POP, POP.*

"There we go!" Cain shouted as the engine roared to life.

He didn't even give them a chance to put on their seat belts. He put the pedal to the metal, and with a shriek of his tires, they were out of the parking lot, and on the fiery road to Hell.

Chapter Nine

"So if he can travel through electrical wires, how can we outrun him?" Tommy asked.

The world flew by them in kaleidoscopes of houses and stoplights and kids on skateboards. Mentally, Mick counted the seconds that had passed since Cain had floored it out of the parking lot: 210. Despite her fear, and her pure outrage at being squeezed into the backseat between Tommy and bags of sweaty gym clothes, Mick was grateful to count every one of them.

"We can't," Cain said. "We have to figure out a way to stop him."

Tanner's face flickered through Mick's mind like a photograph in an album. "Or more people will die."

Tommy exhaled, staring out the window. His voice cracked as he spoke. "This really sucks, you guys."

Cain glanced at him in his rearview mirror. "Don't hurt yourself."

"What?" Tommy asked, spreading his hands. "I'm only stating the obvious. This blows. How was I supposed to know that you had an evil video game? Why would you even have an evil video game?"

"We've been over this already," Cain said.

"Well, I'm going to need you to explain it to me again," Tommy quipped, his hands closing into fists. "Explain why you so casually asked your friend to bring a *DEADLY. VIDEO GAME.* to a public place! Why didn't you wait to exchange it after work? Why did you leave it there on the counter?"

Mick elbowed him. "Cool it."

"I didn't kill anyone," Tommy snapped, crossing his arms. His voice softened as his eyes widened to moons, moved by the pools of water within them. "I didn't kill anyone."

Mick swallowed. If Tommy's face was a watercolor, his agony was the paintbrush. She couldn't look at him for too long without needing to glance out the window. Equally uncomfortable, Cain said nothing, and signaled to make his next turn at a stoplight.

"Mick, you have to believe me. I wouldn't have done this if I knew—if I had ..."

She knew what he was asking even though the words wouldn't form on his lips. He wanted her to know that he didn't mean to kill Tanner. And while she knew, objectively, that CodeSkull had killed her best friend, there was still the underlying problem: Tommy had been so hellbent on owning them during a prank, that he had put their lives at risk. Then again, how was Tommy supposed to have known? And if she was going to think that he was responsible, wouldn't that mean Cain was responsible too?

And her, for putting the game on Tanner's computer? Tanner, who hadn't even wanted to play the game?

Cowardice gnawed at the edges of her conscience. She refused to acknowledge Tommy, continuing to stare out the window. She wouldn't see the defeated look on his face, wouldn't see the way that his hand wiped at his eyes and see the silent prayer he mouthed to himself.

Cain drummed his fingertips against the steering wheel. "Mick, where do you live?"

"Why?" Mick asked.

"Because I'm taking you home?"

"When did we decide on that?" Mick shook her head. "As if. That monster killed my best friend. I'm not going home until he's dead and gone."

"We barely made it out of there alive," Cain said. "And you want to—what, exactly?"

"Surely you had a plan, right?" Mick leaned forward over the driver's center console, pulling her seatbelt to its absolute limits. She gripped one hand on the back of the driver's seat, using it to hold her weight. "That's why you asked your friend to bring you the game?"

"Uh, yeah, that was before people plugged it into a computer and unleashed it upon the town." Cain snorted. "I'm not sure what you think I'm going to do *now*."

Mick's jaw dropped. "You're joking, right?"

"Damn, girl, you're yelling *right* in my ear. Sit your ass back down."

"I'm not yelling—Tommy, tell him I'm not yelling."

"You *both* yell," Cain grumbled. "One of you can't vouch for the other."

"You can't take me home," Mick said. "We have to have a plan."

"That's for me to figure out."

"You can't do this alone! You have to have someone watch your back," Mick said. "Are you delusional?"

"Are *you?*"

Mick smacked her fist into her palm. "A plan, guys, come on; we need a plan!"

Tommy shook his head. "Cain already said what we needed to do."

"What?" Mick whipped her head to face him, her eyes wide. "What do you mean? When?"

"Uh ..." Cain's grip tightened on the steering wheel. "Guys?"

Mick didn't even wait for the command that followed. *Look.* Because she was already staring out the front windshield, up at the traffic lights that hovered menacingly over their intersection. Green. She glanced at the ones to the right side of the road, which controlled the opposite flow of traffic.

Also green.

The Sedan in the lane beside them inched forward as a semi-truck raced through, t-boning the driver. The crash that followed was earth shattering. Metal splintered in all directions and glass exploded like fireworks. Smoke rose up from the exhaust. But even the horrible accident they had witnessed didn't churn their stomachs as much as what came next.

The individual pixels on the traffic light started to flicker and reshape themselves until seconds later, they were staring up at CodeSkull.

"He found us!" Mick shrieked. "Cain, go! Go, go, go!"

Cain hit the accelerator. Horns blared all around them as they waved through traffic. Tires screeched against the asphalt as cars careened and swerved to avoid them. Mick and Tommy each clung to the back of the front seats' headrests, gritting their teeth as they felt the vehicle rumble and roar beneath them. Mick's seatbelt was pulled so tight that it could have sawed through her skin. Cain swore as he spun the wheel, twisting the car out of the way of oncoming traffic. Mick's stomach churned and she resisted the urge to belch as the swerving vehicle righted itself once more. Cain gripped onto the grab handle above him and whooped, throwing back his head.

"How 'bout that?" he shouted to them. "I've only had my license for three weeks!"

But as soon as they thought they were in the clear, a thunderous *POP* echoed out. Were she not so terrified, Mick would've thought it was comical: it almost sounded like a video game explosion, it was so sudden and loud. Both of Cain's hands snapped back to the steering wheel. *POP!* With wary eyes, Mick turned her head to look outside. The powerlines running around the road were starting to blow, green sparks flying everywhere. The fuses on the transformers were snapping one by one as they raced along the county road.

"Cain!" Tommy cried out. "Go faster!"

"Uh, I still have to steer, Tommy!" Cain gritted his teeth as he accelerated through another green-skull light, narrowly avoiding a few other confused cars that had entered the intersection. *POP, POP, POP!* "Y'all want to be helpful? You come up with a plan!"

City buildings and traffic lights soon melted away as they proceeded down the scenic drive of a neighborhood; quaint houses cozied up unsuspectingly underneath power lines that continued to explode into green fireworks. Children playing in driveways screamed in terror and sprinted for the safety of their homes, abandoning their bikes and scooters in the street—

—except for one boy, straddling his 10 speed in the middle of the road, who froze like a deer in headlights.

The three of them screamed as Cain slammed his foot down on the brake, the car skidding to a steamy stop mere inches from the boy. As Cain rolled down his window to demand what the hell was wrong with the kid who so uselessly waited for his own demise, Tommy and Mick continued to watch the power lines explode around them.

"We're sitting ducks!" Tommy cried out, covering his ears.

"If running away doesn't work …" Mick's eyes scanned the tastefully manicured lawns in search of something, anything that was useful. She spotted the house to the left of the car. Huddled together on the front porch were a couple of kids in bathing suits; they couldn't have been any older than seven. Wide-eyed they clung to each other, frozen to their spots, watching as the chaos unfolded around them. Laying on the lawn, right beside their still-spraying sprinkler, were a few Super Soakers. And as she surveyed their neon green-and-yellow plastic bodies, an idea sparked to Mick's mind.

"Get out of the car," Mick said to Tommy, unbuckling her seatbelt.

"What—but he's right out there!"

Mick threw open the door and sprinted outside, making a beeline for the water gun. A series of cracks echoed behind her, and she twisted her head over her shoulder to look. The individual cables had begun snapping off of the powerlines, buzzing and glowing with electric green energy. They unfurled like vipers, slowly extending their long bodies, slithering through the air as though weightless. Mick picked up one of the guns, aimed, and pumped—only to discover that there was no water in it. The kids on the porch began to scream at her as the cables drew closer, and Cain and Tommy shouted for her to return to the car.

Mick glanced at the sprinkler, which was still attached to the hose. She unscrewed the attachment, freeing the spout. Cracking open the gun's seal, she poured more water into the vessel, but she didn't even wait until it was full. One of the cables was close enough to lick her feet. She pumped the gun once more and pulled the trigger. Water sprayed through the nozzle with surprising violence, striking the cable. The cable snapped back, as though offended. As it ventured forward yet again, Mick pulled the trigger, spraying it with a torrent of mist. The cable whipped from side to side, recoiling and curling around itself as it slithered back to the powerline.

"Grab your guns!" she shouted to the boys in the car.

To their credit, Cain and Tommy wasted no time in exiting the vehicle and picking up the remaining water guns on the lawn. The three of them stood shoulder to shoulder, pumping and shooting water at the cables, forcing it back to the power line. When they were no more than a few feet from it, Mick tilted her gun back, aimed for the transformer, and pulled. A cacophony of booms and hisses erupted from the metallic canister, and neon green lit up the sky. Smoke swirled upwards in curls and ribbons of gray and black, and an acrid metallic stench wafted through Mick's nostrils, causing her eyes to water.

As they watched the green sparks recede from the power lines, they kept their guns locked and loaded. When the last of the green sparks had fizzled out, and the cables hung limply in the wind, they finally relaxed. Behind them, they could hear the joyous screams and cheers of the kids, who were now scrambling back out into their yards. All around them, the green sparks were fading from the power lines.

It appeared that CodeSkull had retreated.

But for how long?

Chapter Ten

"Maybe that was it," Tommy suggested. "A few little squirts of water and we sent him running for the hills. Or—well, I guess running isn't the right phrase."

The three of them were now seated inside the local Taco Bell, seated beside the weirdly geometric wall decor. Zigzags and circles piled on top of each other in shades of yellow, purple, peach, and some kind of green that Mick and Tanner could never describe. After leaving the neighborhood, they decided that they needed to regroup, and as Tommy put it, "refuel after the scariest stuff I have ever been through in my life."

Mick slurped on her Mountain Dew and took another bite of her gordita supreme. Though the food was nourishing and delicious, she couldn't help but think of Tanner. On occasion the two of them would bike over here for lunch before heading to Gearscore for an afternoon of kicking ass and taking names. Tanner always insisted on getting the extreme nachos, complete with fiery red chips and a spicy salsa that would always send her to the bathroom for at least forty five minutes after eating. It would always embarrass Mick to no end, and the last time that it happened, she insisted that they go to someplace like Wendy's instead for lunch—at least that way they could get Frostys. But as ridiculous as it was, Mick would give anything to be frustrated with her now, to feel hot-pink embarrassment seeping into her cheeks as she'd wait for her friend in the middle of a crowded restaurant. Prior to Tanner's passing, Mick had no frame of reference for grief. It was not the teeth clenching pain that she had been promised, like a hangnail that had been ripped down to the first knuckle, but instead a haze of melancholy and foolishness, like a fog machine in a haunted house without any visitors. By the time that Cain came and sat down at their table, with his own plate of extreme nachos, Mick felt both like laughing and crying. So she did.

"You okay?" Cain asked. She wondered how someone almost as young as her could speak so seriously. He had such a deep voice and Tommy's register was so close to her own.

Mick wiped at her face. "I'm alright. Sorry for bugging."

"You not bugging," he told her, then looked at Tommy. "What'd you do?"

"Me?" Tommy gaped. "I didn't do anything!"

"Why is she sitting here crying, then?"

"I don't know! Ask her!"

"It's just—my friend," Mick said, stammering between bouts of laughter and sobs. "She loved the extreme nachos."

Cain smiled. "I love 'em, too."

"The Enchirito is the bomb. You guys are missing out," Tommy said, crunching down into his own food, red sauce dribbling down his face. He used a fistful of napkins to clean himself and smacked his lips together, satisfied. "If you want a bite, let me know."

"That's not even supposed to be on the menu anymore," Cain said. "They cut it a few years ago."

"It's on the *secret* menu now," Tommy replied. "I can show you how to order it sometime."

"Hard pass," Cain said. "I'm not a fan of diced onions."

"Diced onions? You have a mysterious salsa on your plate and chips using some kind of random-ass dye, but diced onions is where you draw the line?"

Cain leaned across the table until he was inches from Mick's face. He lowered his voice. "Has he always been this goddamn annoying?"

Mick smiled as she took another sip from her drink. "He's a man of many talents."

"Indeed I am." Tommy took another bite of his burrito, his curious eyes flickering between the two of them. "So, not to harsh your mellow, guys, but what are we thinking? Is he gone?"

Cain sighed as he crunched into a chip. After a long pause, he shook his head.

"No?" Tommy spread his hands. "Why no?"

"Because he's an evil entity that's existed for, like, eons," Cain said. "I think we startled him—maybe I'll be optimistic and even say that we hurt him—but it's going to take a little more than water to defeat him for good."

Mick pressed her face into her hands, taking a deep breath. Of course, she knew it shouldn't have been that simple, and she had suspected as much, but hearing it confirmed by Cain out loud made her feel so much worse. She wanted to avenge Tanner—wanted to prevent this from happening to other kids—but surviving that last situation had been pure dumb luck. How were they, three teenagers armed with super soakers they took from first graders, going to defeat an evil entity who had the power to travel through and control anything electric?

"Tommy." Mick drummed her fingers against the table. "When we were in the car, you said something."

"I say a lot of things, you're going to have to be more specific than that."

"You said …" She snapped her fingers. "You said Cain already said what we needed to do to defeat the monster."

"Ohh, right. Well …" Tommy wiped at his mouth again. The red sauce had stained his lips. "Cain mentioned that everything in this town is connected to the power plant, right? The one off the highway?"

"Yes …?" Mick said, squinting.

"So all we gotta do is shut down the power plant, right?" Tommy spread his hands, his tone so nonchalant Mick would've thought he was stating a fact, like mustard belongs on a hot dog. "If he travels through electricity, once we shut it down, he'll die, right?"

"He won't *die* if he's disconnected from electricity or if the power is shut off," Cain said. "Remember: he *possesses* electrical objects. He's not electricity itself, and it's not his lifesource. He'd still exist in that object, with or without power. And with his abilities, I mean, I think he'd still be a threat."

Tommy sliced into another gooey bite of Enchirito. "Ahh, but he can't go anywhere else, right? He'll be isolated to our grid, and he'll have nowhere to go."

"But what's to stop him from jumping to another grid and spreading to another town?" Mick asked.

Cain shook his head. "Wildwood's power grid is completely independent. I can't believe I'm saying this, but I think Tommy's right. If we shut down the power plant, I don't think CodeSkull will have anywhere to go."

"So how do we get to the power plant without luring him in?" Mick asked.

"We don't." Cain sighed. "Somehow, some way, he's going to know where we are. Which means that if we go to the power plant, we're running the risk that we lose and …"

And he connects to everything. Mick trembled in her seat. CodeSkull could blow the entirety of Wildwood to smithereens. There would be no escape from him. He could utilize enough power that he could be everywhere and in everything, all at once.

"No," Mick said. "We can't. We have to think of another way. If he's afraid of water, what if we crack open a fire hydrant and use a hose to blast him with it?"

"Electricity travels really fast, remember? He could be in another utility pole faster than I can say 'Mississ ippi.'"

"Like I said," Cain said, "I think the water is a temporary thing. It helps, and we'll carry around the water guns with us for sure, but I don't think it's a permanent solution—not to mention, if we get an electrical object wet and then touch it, we're putting ourselves at risk. We should try to get some baking soda or fire extinguishers or something. Right now, I think CodeSkull's weak and probably trying to relearn how his powers work. But demons thrive on chaos. The more chaos he indulges in, the more powerful he becomes. Maybe he was holding back this time, I don't know. But I don't think he'll hold back again."

"And remember those cables?" Tommy added. "He basically has fricking telekinesis. Anything that's electrical, I think he can uproot and use like a sock puppet."

"Or a weapon," Cain said. "More accurately, a weapon."

"Right, right."

Mick slapped her hands against the table. "I'm not convinced of this plan. First of all, how are we even going to get into the power plant? What are we going to do once we successfully shut the plant down? How do we figure out where he's at once we cut him off from the grid?"

"We could lure him to a computer or a phone in there," Cain said. "There's a receptionist's desk that's closed off from the other computers and control systems in the place. That could be a good option."

Mick arched a brow. "How do you know all of this?"

"Because my dad works there. He's an electrical engineer," Cain said. He crunched down on another chip. "And I've gone on the tours. They didn't take y'all there in the fifth grade or whatever?"

"No," Tommy said. "Man, the older kids got to do so much cooler stuff than we do."

Mick shook her head. "Wait, so how are we going to get in? Are you going to ask your dad to let us in?"

Cain scoffed. "Hell no. My dad ain't going to let me into the power plant. He'll think it's weird."

"Really? What if you framed it like a father-son bonding moment?"

"First of all, my dad wasn't born yesterday, and second, I can't pass it off like that with you two knuckleheads tagging along with me. He's going to know something's up."

"Okay." Mick sighed. "So how are we going to get into the power plant?"

"So the power plant uses a keycard security system," Cain said. "My dad always keeps an extra card in the garage, in case he misplaces the one that he keeps in his car."

"So if we steal your dad's keycard, we can get in ourselves?" Mick asked.

Cain nodded.

Tommy munched on the last bite of his Enchirito. "Wicked."

Chapter Eleven

After finishing lunch, they piled into Cain's car once again and headed for his house. Cain lived in a neighborhood adjacent to the center of Wildwood, one which mostly consisted of cozy bungalows and tight, neatly trimmed yards. They were the kind of houses that Mick had driven past with her mother when on the way home from the grocery store, the ones that she had so deeply envied as compared to their dreary split-level rambler with the puke-orange siding. Cain's house had buttercream yellow siding and stretches of wildflowers laid out in front, and their smell invigorated Mick, filling her nostrils as they walked from the driveway through the front door, water guns in hand.

As they walked inside, they were met by more pleasant smells: lavender, as though wafting from fresh laundry.

"Come on." Cain motioned for them to follow, and so they did, after removing their shoes. They proceeded down the steps into an industrial looking basement, which was home to a couple of laundry machines that had seen better days, along with an ironing board that sported a series of interesting scorch marks. Cain's grip tightened around his water gun as he approached a breaker box on the opposite wall from where they stood.

"Be ready for anything," he told them, inching closer to the panel.

Mick and Tommy readied their weapons in response. Grimacing, Cain reached one free hand into the utility sink, and withdrew a rubber glove, which was thankfully dry. He slipped it over his hand, then carefully pried open the breaker box door and flipped all of the switches.

Tommy nodded. "Smart."

"Yep." Cain shut the door to the box, then looked down at his glove. "Huh. I think I'm going to keep this." He reached into the sink and grabbed the other glove, sliding it on. "Don't let me forget to turn it on again;

my mama'll be *pissed* if she comes home to find that the fridge is off. But this way we can get ready in peace and quiet."

Now a little more relaxed, the three of them trudged back upstairs and down another hallway leading to a staircase that reeked of lemon furniture polish (Mick knew the scent because Grandma Lucy used the same one). The hallway itself was a sweet, sunshine yellow that almost matched the outside of the house. Mick noticed all the family portraits arranged on the wall: Cain with his piercings removed and eye makeup wiped clean; a little version of himself sitting on his dad's shoulders. The sweetness of the family photos reminded her of the ones at Tanner's, and it stirred her stomach a little at the thought.

After heading upstairs, they entered a room that was a little too dark and dank, even for Mick's tastes. Knowing what Cain had said about the key card being kept in the garage, Mick was about to ask why they were there, but she stopped when she gazed upon the plethora of decorations plastered on the walls of his room. Punk paraphernalia from so many different bands, including some that she had never heard of. A framed, wilted cover of *Smash Hits* hung over the center of his twin sized bed. The curly-haired woman posed with a proud expression, full lips slightly parted, the metal from her leather biker cap glinting in the light.

"Who is she?" Mick whispered.

"Poly Styrene. X Ray Spex," Cain replied. "Now ... where is it?"

He snapped open his closet door and flicked on the light, revealing the piles and piles of mess inside, nearly indistinguishable from each other. Boxes of records formed haphazard towers, and piles of unfolded laundry surrounded them. He carelessly threw a pair of spiked boots over one shoulder, hitting Tommy square in the abdomen.

"Hello?" Tommy snorted, sidling up to him. "Do you need help with something?"

"Start digging. I'll let you know when we find it."

Tommy sighed and squeezed in beside him. The two dug and tore through the closet while Mick walked around the room, her gun pointed at the various electrical objects, as though fearful they might spring back to life. In theory, if they turned the power off, CodeSkull wouldn't disappear, but if he had wandered into this house with them, he'd still be present in whichever object he had last occupied before Cain had flipped the breakers.

"Found 'em!"

Mick turned to see Cain clutching a bag full of something colorful. It took her a moment to realize that they were rubber balloons, old and covered in dust. She grinned.

"Water balloons?" she asked.

"Just as a backup!" Cain said. "I don't think we can be too careful. And there's probably baking soda in the pantry downstairs."

With their items gathered, they headed back downstairs and into the kitchen to fill up the balloons. Cain retrieved a half-full box of baking soda from a cupboard and placed it into a plastic bag he grabbed from under the sink. Then Tommy tasked himself with filling and tying off each water balloon. Reluctantly, they then split up, with Cain and Mick heading into the garage. As Cain flicked on the light, unveiling a small workshop area and cardboard boxes with water damaged labels, Mick felt a deep sense of uselessness wash over her. Here Cain was, so prepared and knowledgeable in this sea of chaos, and she felt adrift.

"Mick?"

Mick's attention snapped back to Cain, who was holding his weapon, his mouth strung as tight as a clothesline. Panic steeped into her chest like poisonous tea. It must have been visible on her face as well, because Cain shook his head as though to discourage her.

"We're not doing all that," he told her. "Come on. I need your help finding this key card."

She nodded, then got to work, pulling open drawers and cracking open dusty toolboxes. Her fingers threaded strands of cleanliness through thick blankets of sawdust on the shelves, as though trying to scrape up something—anything. She turned her attention to a locked drawer in the rusty metal desk.

"You know where the key to this is?" she asked Cain.

Cain bit his lip, shaking his head. "I don't know."

"Well, where does your dad like to keep important things?"

"Probably on his nightstand, up in my parents' room," Cain said. "Come on, let's go."

They shuffled back into the house, only to discover an odd scene: Tommy, his back pressed against the kitchen sink, the water still running. Piles of shimmering, damp water balloons rested in the sink.

And the fridge, now sparkling with green electricity, had been pulled halfway out of the wall, its long cord wrapped up beside it like a viper.

Chapter Twelve

T ommy shrieked as the fridge snapped forward. The floors quaked beneath them and the vibration was so powerful that it, in fact, rattled the dust off of the light fixture over the dining room table. Although bulky and not quick, it didn't need to be—there was such a narrow pathway from where Tommy stood to the exit that it was going to be difficult for him to escape.

Reaching back, Tommy's shaking hand closed around a water balloon, and he whipped it at the fridge. It shattered on impact, water and sinews of rubber exploding against the plastic doors. But unfortunately, that wasn't enough for CodeSkull, which continued to snap and shake, inching closer.

"What the heck?" Mick cried out. "We flipped the breaker!"

"Well, our worst fears were confirmed: as long as he's in an electrical object, he'll stay alive, power or no power," Cain snapped. "And now we know that he can manipulate the electrical power in an object, regardless if it's connected to a power source."

Mick leaped into action, taking aim at the power cords in the wall and spraying it. The electrical outlet fizzled and popped, but the green glow of the fridge grew brighter. The power was out. CodeSkull had nowhere to run, and nowhere to hide. Unfortunately for them, that didn't work out in their favor—and even worse, they had confirmed their worst fears: that the water at best would only temporarily disable him, but not deter or hurt him.

"It's not working!" Tommy screamed. "Why isn't it working?"

Terrified, he whipped another water balloon at the fridge. Cain reached into his back pocket for the box of baking soda, removed a fistful of it, and chucked it at the monster, but it wasn't enough to subdue the monstrous fridge. The pathway from the sink to the exit had only gotten narrower, and at this point, there was no way that Tommy could run out, even if he wanted to.

"Tommy!" Mick cried out. "You're going to have to jump!"

"Jump *where*?"

Mick slapped the surface of the countertop. The fridge seemed to tilt in her direction, as though acknowledging her plan, but Tommy moved faster. He dived towards the countertop, swinging his legs up and over, and falling unceremoniously on the other side. Cain and Mick quickly helped him to his feet, and the three screamed as the unthinkable happened.

The fridge *jumped.*

The cord, tingling with green electricity, snapped taut and tight as the hunk-of-metal monster lurched forward, colliding with the counter. *BOOM!* The metal crushed the Formica surface, flattening it to the ground the way Mario would a Goomba. Splinters of wood ricocheted through the air and across the kitchen floor. Crushed ceramic shards scattered everywhere, and the kitchen tiles crunched into pulverized, dusty little pieces.

Cain's hands tangled in his hair as he unleashed a primal scream. "Oh my GODDDDDDDD!"

"I know!" Tommy cried out. "I almost crapped my pants!"

"You asshole!" Cain threw another fistful of baking soda at the fridge, little white pellets sizzling. "You're going to make me explain this to my *MAMA*?"

The fridge snapped forward again, straining its cord, and the kids shrieked, leaping out of its path. They backed away, arms interlocked and guns aimed, watching to see what it would do. CodeSkull rocked from side to side on the floor, furthering the damage to the surrounding counters.

"Yo!" Cain barked at the fridge, angrier than he was afraid. "You stop that right now!"

Tommy lowered his gun for a second, his mouth screwed in a confused frown. "What is it *doing?*"

Mick watched as it continued to repeat the motion, over and over again. Each time, it seemed to be getting more air. Her eyes widened.

"Guys, it's trying to *stand up again,*" she cried out, shoving them towards the hallway. "Cain, go, we have to go! We have to find that keycard!"

The three of them sprinted up the stairs, the crunching-rocking motions of CodeSkull thundering throughout the house. Cain led the way into his parents' bedroom, and Tommy threw the door shut, then locked it. Mick shot him a look.

"What?" Tommy demanded. "It's for good measure."

"Can a fridge climb stairs even if it wanted to?"

"Hold that thought, Mick," Cain said, wrenching open his dad's nightstand drawer. "Hold it, because I don't even want to think about it!"

Wasting no time, Cain turned the drawer upside down and emptied all its contents. Coins bounced onto the carpet, along with random discarded buttons, their stray pieces of thread blending in with its shaggy strands. Wallets, worn by time. A container of heartburn medication. Suspiciously rusty toenail clippers. A couple of condoms, which led to all three of them screaming even more. And finally, a tiny spare key, its plastic bow cracked and filled with dirt—something that damningly belonged to the drawer outside, based on its size, shape, and condition.

"Found it!" Cain cried out, pinching the key between his fingers and holding it up to the light.

All around them, the house continued to rumble with the ferocity of an earthquake. Mick felt like she was being squished between two cymbals; it was so loud and violent. Another thunderous *CRASH!* echoed out, shaking the ground beneath their feet. Tommy unlocked the door and raced into the hallway, gun pointed.

"Oh you're freaking kidding me!" he howled.

Cain and Mick joined him shortly after. The fridge had crushed the bottom of the stairs. Spiderwebs of cracks continued up the walls to the second floor. Cain's jaw hung open, and, for a moment, Mick was worried it'd be stuck like that permanently. She shook him and he remained frozen to the spot as if overwhelmed by the destruction that had been brought upon his home. But at this point, Mick wasn't worried as much about the destruction as she was about the outcome. Maybe CodeSkull couldn't climb the stairs in that body, but the longer that they stayed in this house, the more damage that he could do. If CodeSkull took out a load bearing wall, it was game over. Cain's sweet and quaint home would become nothing more than a death trap.

"We have to get out of here," Mick said, squeezing Cain's shoulder. "Is there an exit?"

"On the second floor of the dang house?" Tommy muttered, casting Mick severe side-eye.

Mick ignored him. "Cain! A trellis! A window! Anything?"

Cain motioned for them to follow him into his room once more. He climbed onto his bed, wrenched open the window, and gestured to what lay below—a bed of bushes.

Tommy's jaw dropped. "You don't even climb a *gutter*, man?"

"No," Cain said. "Just get out, hang, and drop."

"Get out, hang, and drop," Tommy muttered to himself. "Well, I guess it's better than being in here."

He swung his leg over the edge of the windowsill. Gritting his teeth, he then moved his other leg, trying to twist his body to face the correct way around. Whimpering, he lowered his body down the side of the house, the window creaking underneath his weight. His fingers clawed at the sill. He muttered a prayer underneath his breath in Spanish, then let go. He collided with the bushes on the bottom, falling back on his ass, the branches splaying every which way. After a moment of groaning, he held his thumb up.

"Mick," Cain said. "You go next."

Mick nodded. She climbed over the side of the window, and as soon as she did, CodeSkull sent another *BOOM* echoing through the house. Within seconds, Mick lost her grip, and she yelped. As she fell, she stared up into Cain's worried eyes, his mouth hung open in shock. She collided not with branches, but with something soft.

"Gotcha!" Tommy cried out, his arms wrapping around her. "Cain! I got her! She's good!"

Mick and Tommy scrambled to their feet, crawling out of the bushes. As they picked twigs and leaves off each others' bodies, Cain also dropped. *SMASH!* The three exchanged a look with each other, but instinctively knew they had no time to investigate the ominous sound. They sprinted for the garage, wrenching open the door, and stumbled back towards the drawer in the workshop. Cain fumbled around in his pockets, turning them inside out. His skin grayed, ashen with fear.

"What's wrong?"

"I think it—" his voice dropped to a whisper, panic seeping in. "I think it fell out of my pocket when I landed in the bushes."

"Step aside," Tommy said, nudging him away.

He reached for a pair of scissors, spreading them open. Then he jammed one end into the lock. He glanced back at them, grabby-hands motioning for assistance.

"Paperclip! Bobby pin! Anything!"

Cain scrambled for the other end of the table, sliding open a top drawer. He fumbled through the dust and random junk pieces and procured a small and rusted paperclip. He passed it to Tommy. Tommy unpeeled one end of the paperclip from the body, extending it until it formed two hooked ends. He inserted the paperclip above the edge of the scissors and then started to work his magic. Within seconds, the drawer popped open, and there it was.

The keycard.

"Yoink!"

Tommy snatched up the card, and the three of them cheered, slapping high fives. They scrambled out of the garage. Sweat rolled down Mick's forehead, and she wiped it away with the back of her hand. As they approached Cain's car, they all came to a sudden stop, their joy evaporating like spoiled milk under the summer sun.

"Hey guys," Tommy said. "Is it just me or is it *super* quiet now?"

Cain and Mick exchanged apprehensive expressions before turning and twisting every which way to look at their surroundings. Most of the surrounding homes were at peace, their garage doors shut, the front yards eerily quiet and absent of children—then again, Mick supposed that Cain could've lived in a neighborhood where kids weren't around. But then she saw the giant, rectangular hole where the front door used to be.

"Oh my God," she gasped. "He escaped."

"And went where, exactly?" Tommy asked.

Somber, Cain lifted his hand and pointed to the house next door. A fridge, irreparably dented and covered in shrapnel of all different materials, had backed itself up against the house's electricity meter.

Within seconds, their world was green again.

Chapter Thirteen

"You've got to be kidding me!" Cain roared, slamming the heel of his hand against the steering wheel.

They were racing through the streets once again, weaving and dodging the exploding streetlights. Although the situation was as high octane as ever, Mick couldn't help but feel numb. They had gotten the key card, but Cain's house had been destroyed, their water guns were at least halfway depleted, and they didn't even have any of the water balloons that Tommy had prepared. At best, they had half a box of baking soda that'd be gone in five seconds. They were, as Tanner would have so eloquently put it, "up shit creek without a paddle."

"For what it's worth," Tommy called from the backseat, "you're doing great, Cain."

"Thanks, Tommy!" Cain gritted his teeth in a half-hearted smile as he careened around the corner. He slammed his fist on the horn, dodging a passing vehicle that had suddenly spun out of control when it saw the flashing green lights. "You killed it back there! Where the hell did you learn how to pick a lock? Why didn't you do that earlier?"

Tommy's cheeks darkened. "My mom loses the keys to her jewelry box all the time. Had to figure out a solution. I only knew how to pick that one lock—we're lucky I could do it for that drawer."

"Damn! Here's to moms losing their shit, I guess. Kinda like how my mom is going to lose her shit when this is all over!"

Tommy nudged Mick. "Hey, you okay? You look a little pale."

"I'm fine," Mick said, the words like ice on her tongue. Ice would feel good about now. Applied to her still-perspiring forehead or to the joints that were still throbbing from her fall onto Tommy. *Wait.* She looked at Tommy. "You're okay, right?"

He rolled up the end of his shirt, unveiling a myriad of bruises. "I mean, I don't think I've sprained a rib or anything, so that's a bonus, right? It doesn't hurt to breathe." He took a deep breath as though to demonstrate. "See?"

"Oh my God," Mick whispered, her eyes welling with tears.

True, it wasn't that bad of an injury—maybe it would clear up in the next few days—but for some reason, seeing Tommy like this was enough to send her over the edge. Tears sprung from her eyes as though they were little people fleeing a burning building. As suburbia peeled away and the farmlands surrounding the county road faded into existence, Cain pulled the car off to the side of the road, safely away from the power lines.

"Mick," Cain said. "You gotta get a grip, girl."

Tommy was more soothing. "Mick, Mick, I'm fine. Really. It hurts but I've had worse. You should hear about the time that I visited my abuelita in Tibasosa and her horse kicked me in the ass. I literally couldn't sit for two days straight."

Mick snorted with laughter. Snot dripped from her nose. Tommy tore off the end of his tattered shirt and offered the piece to her. She used it to wipe at her face for a few moments, until she realized that it was greasier than using her own hands.

"Yuck," she said, dropping it to the floor.

"Don't leave your snot rag on the floor of my car."

Mick chuckled, scooping up the scrap, and tossing it outside. Tears continued to roll down her cheeks, soothing and cool.

"This is wack," Cain said.

"Wack," Tommy agreed.

"I don't blame you for feeling the way you do," Cain said. "But you wanted to come along on this adventure. I don't think you can turn back now."

"No," Mick said, her voice hoarse. "I can't."

"Yeah, so ..." Cain stared out the window, his fingers tapping rhythmically against the dash. *Boo-BOOM, boo-BOOM, boo-BOOM.* "What's going on? What's hitting you so hard, and why now?"

"I feel ..." *Useless.* She couldn't even form the word on her lips.

"Feel what?"

"I feel useless," she said finally, tremors coursing through her body. "T-Tommy knows how to lockpick and he filled up the water balloons, and Cain knows so much about *everything,* and I'm the one who played the stupid game to begin with. I'm the one who caused all of this. I'm the reason why Tanner is dead. Because I couldn't let a stupid rivalry go."

Both boys shook their heads. Mick continued to cry, not hiding her face, but wiping her eyes over and over again, as her chin and lip continued to wobble, as she gritted her teeth to prevent the sob from escaping. The noise boiled down to a primal whimper yearning to turn into a howl. Crying was the last thing she ever, ever wanted to do—especially in front of Tommy Perlaza.

But he gently rubbed her shoulder in response, shaking his head. "That's not true, Mick."

"Yeah. The hell?" Cain scoffed. "You better get that out of your head. If it's anyone's fault, it's mine. Or my friend's for bringing the game to me. Or to whoever trapped the damn demon in that floppy disc in the first place instead of just throwing salt on him or some shit. It's a whole line-up of mistakes that got us into this mess. But it is not your fault. You had no idea what you were dealing with."

"It's my fault," Tommy whispered. "Because I shouldn't have stolen the game."

"No—would the two of you get a grip?" Cain unbuckled his seatbelt so that he could fully twist around and face them. He pointed a stern finger in each of their faces. "It's. No one's. Fault. Okay? It's no one's fault. And that kind of thinking doesn't do any good, and worse, it's going to eat you alive. Let me ask you this, Mick. You believe in heaven? You believe in an afterlife?"

Mick had never thought about that before. Her family didn't really attend church. They were a mass-on-Easter-Sunday kind of family, and to tell the truth, Mick didn't even know what denomination they belonged to. Probably Catholic? She didn't know. It wasn't that important to her in the grand scheme of things and not that important to her parents. But she did believe in ghost stories, and she did believe that when she buried her turtle Franklin in the third grade that he had gone to turtle heaven, where he could eat as many dried shrimp as he wanted and sunbathe on the warmest, coziest rocks.

"I'd like to," she admitted.

"So you think that Tanner is sitting up there in heaven going, damn, that was Mick's fault. Because if I died and I was looking down at my friend, you know what I'd be thinking?" His voice softened. "'I hope she's okay. I hope she makes it out alive.' That's all she's thinking right now, guarantee it."

Mick cracked a smile as more tears rolled down her cheeks. "She's probably sitting on a chaise lounge getting fed grapes by like, eight different Liu Kang clones."

"Who?" Cain asked, arching a brow.

"The super hot guy from *Mortal Kombat* with the long, luscious locks," Tommy said.

Cain's brows rose further as he switched his gaze over to Tommy. "*You* think he's hot?"

Rather than outright deny it, Tommy screwed his mouth in a frown, deeply considering it. After a moment he said, "I mean, yeah. I'm not blind."

"Alright. That's cool, I guess." Cain cracked his neck from side to side, looking back at Mick. "And what's this about feeling useless? You saved Tommy's ass back at the video store. You're the one who had the bright idea to start using squirt guns on him, something that I didn't even think of first. Honestly, I'm still pissed that I didn't think of it first, but that's alright."

"And you got us away from Fridgemadgeon," Tommy added. "Landing on me instead of the bush is honestly the least I could do."

"Right." Cain chuckled. "Plus it was funny as hell."

For a moment Tommy appeared offended, but he burst into giggles. "Did you see her face on the way down? Her eyes nearly popped out of her head."

Mick elbowed Tommy playfully, and as she did, her tears finally subsided. Her heartbeat slowed, and once more, she felt like she was in control of her emotions. A wide smile broke out across Cain's face.

"Alright?" he said, spreading his hands. "We good?"

"We're good," Mick said.

"I can't *hear* you. Are we good or are we GOOD!" Cain yelled, throwing back his head. "Loud and clear, let me HEAR you!"

"WE GOOD!" Mick and Tommy shouted back.

"AGAIN?!"

"WE GOOD!"

"Damn straight," Cain said, twisting back around and buckling his seatbelt again. "Let's go kick some demon-ass."

Chapter Fourteen

Upon arriving at the power plant, Mick was glad that she had never been there before. As soon as she opened the door and climbed out of Cain's Taurus, the stench of sulfur hit her with the force of a train. It permeated the air like a foul fog. Although the plant was nestled in the cozy hills off the county roads, the surrounding trees were surprisingly dull and wilted for the middle of summer. Jug-shaped towers nestled beneath the clouds in the sky, sunfish in an ocean of blue, white-hot smoke blowing from their open mouths.

Cain stretched his body from side to side. He had gunned it the remainder of the way to the power plant in an attempt to outrun CodeSkull and taken some additional twists and turns to try to throw the demon off. So far, they hadn't encountered any additional exploding lights, so presumably, he was behind them.

But not for long.

Tommy shook his water gun, biting his lip. "Anyone else like halfway out?"

"How the hell are you halfway out when Mick and I were doing all the shooting back at my place?"

Tommy blinked. "So ... your backseat is a little wet."

Cain's jaw dropped. "Tommy, you let your water gun *leak* all over my car?"

"I didn't notice it until I got out." Tommy shrugged his shoulders. "Sorry."

"Ugh. Man. And we don't have water balloons either ..." Mick clicked her tongue against her teeth as her heart rattled the walls of her rib cage. "Maybe there'll be a way that we could fill it up in a bathroom sink."

Cain fished around in his pocket for the key card and held it up. "No time to waste. Let's hurry up."

The parking lot stretched out before them. Presumably, during the day, there would be cars filling up each of the spaces, but since it was after five o'clock, most people had gone home for the day. Most people, except for Cain's dad who tended to work the later shifts. The asphalt desert seemed to only lengthen the further that the group jogged. But as they reached the sidewalk, Mick breathed a sigh of relief.

Only a little further left to go, and hopefully, this would all be over.

The entrance of the power plant was oddly extravagant. Mick had thought the place would be made of boring stuff like stone and brick, but through the floor-to-ceiling windows, she could make out a lobby, with an unoccupied secretary's desk, a pair of elevators, and several hallways branching off into other parts of the facility. Taking it all in, Mick was less impressed and more concerned. How the hell were they going to get to whatever control room would allow them to switch off the electricity? And how were they going to do it before CodeSkull showed up to wreak havoc?

Cain stood in front of an odd black box protruding beside the door. On its surface, a little red light shone, an eye squinting in the light of the summer sun. Cain held up the card and pressed it to the black box. The light flashed, and a buzzer noise echoed out.

"ERROR," said a tinny, robotic voice. Mick then realized that there was a speaker embedded into the black box. "ACCESS DENIED."

"*What?*" Cain cried out, his voice shrill. He scanned it again, only to receive the same error. "I don't—I don't understand!"

"Wait, isn't your dad still inside the building?" Tommy asked.

"Yeah, but—"

"—Yeah, then if he's still inside the building, I think that's why we're getting an error message. You scan once to go in, and once to go back out," Tommy suggested.

"You're telling me that these people *never* hold open the door for their coworkers?" Cain scoffed, ruffling his hair in frustration. "You gotta be kidding me."

"Either that, or maybe this key card has been de-activated," Tommy said. "We're going to need to find another way in."

"What if we drive the car through the window of the lobby?" Mick asked.

"Let's not," Cain said. "I'd rather not lose my car in case we have to make a break for it. And if we don't come up with a plan in the next five seconds, we're going to have to do that." Gritting his teeth, he threw the keycard to the ground. "Useless—all for *nothing!*"

Tommy patted Cain's shoulder, and to Mick's sur-prise, he accepted the affectionate gesture, squeezing his hand in response. She turned and looked around the parking lot. Her friends—if they considered her one after all she'd put them through—thought that she was capable. That she was essential to their cause. She could find another way to prove them right. Scanning the near-empty parking lot, she spotted the car that was closest to them.

"Maybe we don't destroy Cain's car," Mick said, "but what if we mess up someone else's?"

"Explain," Tommy said, rolling his eyes.

"If we set off a car alarm, would someone come running?" Mick asked Cain.

Cain shrugged his shoulders. "Worth a shot."

"Okay. Tommy, you keep trying the key card in case we weren't like, holding it right or something, and Cain, let's make some noise."

Tommy crouched down to retrieve the key card as Cain and Mick jogged over to the nearest car, a Honda Odyssey that smelled like string cheese the closer they got to it. Mick resisted the urge to plug her nose as she started to tug on door handles. To her surprise, the passenger side door opened, unveiling a treasure trove of discarded food wrappers and... *used pantiliners?*

"I'm outtie," Mick said, slamming the door shut. "Who leaves their car door unlocked?"

"Morons," Cain replied. "Then again, who would want to steal this piece of junk?"

WHOMP-WHOMP-WHOMP-WHOMP-WHOMP!

Cain and Mick spun around towards the entrance where a wide-eyed Tommy clutched the key card. The light on the scanner was now flashing red over and over.

"ERROR, ERROR!" the scanner called out between its siren screams. "SECURITY INCOMING. SECURITY INCOMING."

"How come this town got money for a state-of-the-art security system but no damn money for the school library?" Cain muttered as they jogged back over to Tommy. "You know how long I've been waiting for them to get Clive Barker's *Galilee*?"

Tommy gulped nervously, shaking his head as though ashamed. Mick turned and looked into the lobby. A shadowy figure was slowly approaching, their long form stretching across the canvas of blank walls. Swallowing a lump of fear in her throat, Mick realized that they might have blown their only chance.

Chapter Fifteen

T he man who opened the door mere moments later bore a striking resemblance to one of the kids. He had broad shoulders scarcely hidden beneath a white lab coat (perhaps it had been left in the dryer for too long?) and a nose that matched his son's, although his eyes were a different shade of brown. Then again, that could've been a trick of the light, thanks to the large horn-rimmed glasses that occupied most of his face.

"Dad?" Cain said, surprised.

"Micah?" the man asked, equally confused.

"*Micah?*" Mick and Tommy said in unison.

Mr. Williams smiled but was unable to hide the confusion on his face. He arched a brow at his son. "You still telling people your name is *Arcane?*"

"Wait," Tommy said, "you mean your name isn't actually 'Cain?' It's a nickname?"

Flustered, Cain ushered them all inside the building, and somehow, the trio managed to shoulder their way past his father, despite his protests.

"Whoa, whoa, whoa!" he called out, letting the door close behind him, although he kept his hand on the handle, as though prepared to send them back outside. "Timeout. What are you doing here? Who are these kids, Micah? And are those *water guns?*"

"I don't have time to explain, Dad," Cain said. "Any second now, he's going to be here, and we gotta get to the control room before he does."

"He? Who's he?"

Staring past Mr. Williams, Mick watched as green raced up the road, popping all the bulbs in the streetlights. Green fire rained down, littering the asphalt below. She raised her water gun.

"Mr. Cain's dad, sir," Mick said, "take your hand off the handle!"

Tommy and Cain lifted their guns as well, noticing what was going on outside.

"What?" Mr. Williams asked, unimpressed.

"THE DOOR HANDLE!" they screamed at him.

Perplexed, he dropped his hand from the handle. Although Mick had spoken to him first, Mr. Williams' eyes wouldn't leave his son's face. "Micah, son, you better stop this foolishness right now. This is not a place to be playing games at. This is my place of work."

"It's not a game, Dad," Cain cried out. "Dad, get away from the door!"

"I will get away from the door as soon as the three of you get your asses outside," he replied, his voice restrained.

"We can't leave," Mick said, desperation sinking into her voice. "We've got to shut everything down before it's too late! And get away from the door!"

"Alright," his dad said, "I've had *enough*."

"Look!" Tommy screamed in frustration, pointing to the array of exploding lights behind him.

Finally, the man turned to see the dazzling sight behind him. It would've been so pretty if Mick wasn't so terrified. Alarmed, the man stumbled back from the door.

"What in the hell …?" he muttered, raising his glasses as though that would help him see better. "What is going on?"

"It's a demon, Dad," Cain said, exasperated. "There's a demon trapped in the electrical wires of the town, and—"

"Micah, Micah," his dad said, tossing his head, "You know your mom and I love that you're exploring your interests, but I can't deal with the weird stuff right now! There are no ghosts trapped in the wires, or—"

At that moment, CodeSkull entered the door scanner, his green sparks sizzling and sparkling from the cracks and crevices in the little black box. Shouting, the three kids begged his dad to step away—but this time, he didn't.

The explosion that followed was deafening.

Chapter Sixteen

Try as she might, Mick couldn't stop the ringing in her ears. When the scanner had exploded, its internal alarm had released its swan song, cracking the glass and shattering the nearest window. Spiderweb cracks criss-crossed their way across the front lobby. Mr. Williams had managed to turn his back as the explosion had occurred, and his lab coat was now glistening with glass particles; small holes had eaten their way into his clothing like moths. His hands were cupped over his ears, and he gnashed his teeth, tossing his head from side to side. Whether he was in pain from the glass or the noise of the explosion or *both*, Mick didn't know. She was only glad that he was still standing on his own two feet.

"Dad!" Cain cried out, sprinting forward. "Dad, are you okay?"

"I've been better," he grumbled in response, massaging his temples. "What the hell was that?"

"We've been trying to tell you," Tommy said. "It's CodeSkull. The demon that's trapped in the electrical wires."

"Aren't you kids a little too old to believe in demons?"

"*Dad,*" Cain snapped, "is a *door scanner* supposed to explode like that? And what about all the green sparks? Focus!"

His dad arched a brow.

"Focus ... please," Cain corrected himself. "CodeSkull's here, and we have to find a way to stop him before he gets into the electric grid and takes over everything all at once."

"It was malfunctioning equipment," his dad said. "More like overpriced pieces of s—shiitake mushrooms. You know they put this in instead of giving us a Christmas bonus this year?"

Green sparks erupted from the receptionist's computer. All three of the kids gasped, raising their water guns. Mr. Williams, somehow still unconvinced, motioned for them to lower their weapons as he jogged over.

"Now what in the hell is going ..."

He froze, eyes wide, as though he had seen a ghost. Mick knew the feeling. She had felt it the same time she saw that skull pop up on the TVs at Flicks Forever. He cried out in fear as the green flames erupted from the computer, wild and ravenous as a murder of crows. Sparks shot off in multiple directions, and the cord snapped away from its socket, inching closer to the shocked father.

Cain cried out for his dad and lifted his water gun, dousing the computer. Mick winced as it was extinguished. There went their plan to trap CodeSkull in that object. Now what were they going to do? He was mere minutes, possibly seconds, from getting to the mainframe.

"I know you don't believe in the same things I do," Cain said, "but I need you to trust me. We gotta get to the mainframe and power down the grid. It's the only way to save Wildwood."

For the first time since they had encountered him, Mr. Williams dropped his shoulders, softening some of the stern personality that he possessed. He looked between his son and the computer and nodded. He didn't need to say anything else. He motioned for the kids to follow him, and soon their feet were pounding against the ground, as they sprinted down the winding hallways. As they raced along, Mick could hear the buzzing of fluorescent lights in adjacent hallways: CodeSkull was trying to find them. With the size of this place, they might be able to buy a little bit of time. It also dawned on Mick that CodeSkull might not entirely realize what they were trying to do, might not understand that the greatest source of power was located in this building.

Could they actually pull this off?

The deeper that they went into the power plant, the more it started to feel like being lost in a labyrinth. They came to a series of intersecting hallways as plain and abysmal as the rest of the building. Overhead, the lights flickered, then snapped off, suspending them in complete darkness. Mick bumped into someone's sweaty shoulder, and at the sound of his *"Oof,"* realized it was Tommy.

Just as she was about to open her mouth to ask where they were supposed to go, Cain whispered, "Shh! It's looking for us."

Threads of green light swam through the overhead fluorescents like a shark's fin skimming the surface of dark water. Mick watched as small sparkles wandered down an adjacent hallway.

"This way," she heard Mr. Williams say. "Quietly."

They proceeded through the hallways quieter than before, the zipping and crackling of the electric lights close behind. Soon enough, they came to the master control room, hidden behind a pair of doors with oval windows, the kind that Mick would see in every classic sci-fi film. A mysterious blue light beckoned to them through the glass. Mr. Williams fished in his pocket for his keycard and opened the door, ushering them inside. Mick tilted her head, looking up at a series of impressive computer monitors, the source of the blue light. They were stacked together in a 10x10 wall, stretching from one end of the room to the other on top of what appeared to be a massive metal table, decked out with an array of control switches, levers, and buttons. Each of the monitors were nearly twice as big as the Toshiba rear projection TV that sat in Mick's living room. About ten different office chairs, some of which were musty with age and torn from use, occupied the space.

"This is Mission Control," Mr. Williams said.

Squinting at the screens, Mick could see what appeared to be some type of map, constructed from a series of lines and circles and other various symbols. The maps stretched across the entire screen, taking up the entirety of the monitors. She noticed that some of the circles on the map were flashing red.

"What is that supposed to be?" she asked.

"That is an electrical map of Wildwood." Mr. Williams squinted at the array of monitors, raising his glasses from his head. "What in the world ..."

Mick realized that he was looking at all the red dots. "Would that, uh, happen to be the intersection over by the video store, by chance?"

Mr. Williams flicked a button, and a vaguely-transparent image of the town, complete with buildings and street names, snapped over the top of the electrical grid. It reminded Mick of one of the photomontages that she had made in fourth grade art class.

"I don't understand," Mr. Williams muttered. "This has been going on all day?"

"*All* day, Dad," Cain said. "People have died. How did you not know about this?"

Mr. Williams cleared his throat, as though irritated by his son's line of questioning. "Well, I have many things to attend to throughout the day, and for your information, I wasn't on duty for watching the monitors." He shuffled in place, somewhat uncomfortable. "Also, it was Gerald's birthday today and we all went to Applebee's."

"So then *no one* was watching the monitors?" Tommy asked, astounded.

"There should have been at least one person here, and not only that, the emergency alarms should have been working ..." He began typing onto a keyboard on one surface, bringing up a complex black box. "I don't understand."

Mick interjected. "I don't think that it matters now. We gotta get it shut down. Do you know how to do that?"

"To shut down the electrical grid, we need the emergency key." Mr. Williams pointed to a black and yellow striped hazard box in the center of the control unit. A glass cover shielded what appeared to be some sort of keyhole beneath it. "And I can only get it from the previous person on duty."

"Dude," Tommy said, "I feel like I'm playing through the Water Temple level in *Ocarina of Time*. How does this keep getting harder?"

"Are you saying that you want it to be *easier* to turn off the electricity for an entire town?" Mr. Williams replied.

"Dad," Cain asked, "how do we find the emergency key? Do you know who had it?"

"It would've been the previous person on duty. Let me see here ..."

He reached into a compartment below the desk, withdrawing a binder. Each paper he removed appeared to have a complicated schedule on it. As he continued to pore over the schedules, Mick couldn't help but hear the tiny *bzz-bzz* echoing somewhere nearby. She twisted her head around, trying to listen for the noise. Darkness consumed the other half of the room, where the monitors' blue light had faded. Mick crept closer, her water gun lifted. There appeared to be even more controls and complicated machinery on the wall opposite from the doorway they had entered. She realized that she was looking at row after row of servers. *Bzz-bzz.* She guessed it made sense that the electrical power plant would need this many to keep their systems afloat.

Gritting her teeth, Mick lifted her water gun and proceeded into the maze. The giant towers of technology only had small lights, not nearly enough to illuminate the entire space. *BZZ-BZZ.* The further she walked down the row, the louder the noise grew. She didn't notice any green twinkling lights, but something about this felt so off. She couldn't help it when the tremors coursed through her body.

As she rounded another series of corners, she finally found it.

A man's body leaned against the towering severs, a series of cords and cables wrapped around his neck. Blisters and electrical burns, still raw and red, peppered the exposed surfaces of his body. The unmistakable stench of rot and charred flesh eroded Mick's nostrils, simmering in her queasy stomach.

They were too late. And maybe they had been too late all along.

CodeSkull had already been here.

Fear closed its gnarled and nasty teeth around Mick's mind. If CodeSkull had already been here, then why would he have let them walk into this place to begin with? Why had it taken so long for him to catch up with them? As soon as that thought swept in, another one superseded it in a tidal wave of terror.

He wanted to get them alone.

Mick knew she had to act fast. Grimacing, she scanned the dead body. His lab coat was open, the torn pockets inside exposed. She saw something poking out the bottom of one of them—a key with a square peg, its handle in the same black-and-yellow striped colors she saw on the emergency stop button in the control room. Crouching low, she attempted to move close to the body, only to become overwhelmed with the stench. Gagging, Mick slung her water gun to one shoulder, plugged her nose, and used the other to carefully fish the key from the bloodied pocket. As soon as her fingers clasped around it, she wrenched away from the corpse, swallowing back the bile that tried to force its way up her throat.

She sprinted back to the mission control room, and as she broke through the maze of servers, she saw that they were still fumbling through the binders of sched-ules. As she opened her mouth to shout at them, her blood ran cold.

Green had seeped into the computer monitors like spilled ink on paper.

Chapter Seventeen

"Cain! Tommy!" she screeched like she never had before, her lungs and throat ripping from the fiery force of her voice. "He's here! He *knows!*"

Eyes widening, Cain and Tommy whipped around to face the wall of computers. Each pixel turned from blue to green in a vicious tsunami, green sparks flying from the surface of the monitors like spitting seafoam. Immediately Tommy lifted his gun and fired, streams of water blasting the surface of one of the monitors. Not even a little smoke puffed from the monitor's various crevices.

"He lured us here," Mick cried out. "He lured us here so he could ..."

The words stopped in her throat like the bile she had swallowed only moments before. *So he could kill us.* This whole time, CodeSkull had known that they were the greatest threat to his reign of terror. He had known their plan. They had been so foolish. Who were they, a bunch of ragtag teens, to think that they could overcome the might of an ancient demon?

Fireworks erupted from the surface of the monitors, littering the floor below. All of a sudden, Mick felt like she was trapped in a tank full of rising water. As CodeSkull took control of the monitors, the servers also succumbed to his whim. Yelping in fear, they all backed against the wall, trying to maintain as much distance as possible. Electronic whirs and shrill screeches erupted from the servers as one by one, they burst into flame. Smoke filled their nostrils and Mick turned her mouth into her shoulder so she could cough.

"You found it."

Mick turned to look up into Mr. Williams' face, his eyes sparkling with awe. She presented the key to him without a second thought but shook her head in defeat. "But Mr. Williams, isn't it too late?"

"No," Mr. Williams said. "Just because he got access to the system doesn't mean that we can't shut it down. Let me handle this."

"What?" Cain cried out. "Dad, if you go anywhere *near* that thing it will try to kill you."

Mr. Williams glanced at the wall behind him, where a red glass case held a fire extinguisher. He picked up the little hammer, smashed the glass, and withdrew its contents. He shoved the emergency key into his pocket and separated the hose from the body of the extinguisher, stretching it outwards.

"You still got some water left in those guns, right?" Mr. Williams asked them, and they nodded in response. "Then cover me!"

Mr. Williams charged towards the emergency shut-off button. *PING-PING-PING!* CodeSkull's electricity seeped into the surrounding wires and cables, snapping away from the mainframe, the green glow of his life energy overpowering them. One cable retracted and then snapped forward, but a blast of water from Mick's gun was able to hold it back. Mr. Williams danced around the various sparks raining down from the monitors, performing a high-octane tango as he inched closer to the coveted glass case. Foam spat from the extinguisher's hose, coating the floor in a slippery carpet. Tommy and Cain flanked either side while Mick held up the back. One of the cables swam close to her face, its frayed ends reverberating with green violence. She shrieked, narrowly dodging its attempt to slap her, and soaked it with water.

With their guns dwindling, Mick didn't know how much longer they could last, but luckily for them, Mr. Williams had reached the emergency shut-off. He smashed open the cover with the end of the extinguisher, then tossed it to the side. He jammed the key into the system and twisted it. Emergency-red overloaded green on the monitors in a catastrophe of Christmas colors. Mr. Williams barked out a triumphant laugh, throwing his head back. For the briefest of moments, Mick watched as relief flickered across her friends' faces.

Then one cable snapped forward from the dead center of the monitors. It struck with the speed and accuracy of a cobra, punching Mr. Williams square in the throat before wrapping itself around his neck. Gagging, he gripped onto the emergency button in a desperate attempt to hold on, but the demon continued to lift his body from the floor, his wing tipped shoes scraping the tiles below. Mr. Williams was stronger—the muscles and veins in his neck and arms pulling taut and tight, protruding even from the thick fabric of his clothing. But just as it seemed he was about to land back on the ground safely, green lightning flashed through the cable, consuming the man whole.

Mick saw Cain's mouth open but couldn't hear him scream. She suddenly felt like she was trapped in a wind tunnel. Gone were the crackles and sparks, the roars of the flaming servers behind them, the shrill electric screams of the monitors and voices warning that there was an emergency. Overhead, sprinklers popped out from the ceiling, raining down on them. Green and red flashed across the monitors, and the sparks sizzled into smoke. The cable jerked, CodeSkull's power weakening, until finally, he dropped Mr. Williams; his body falling to the ground in a limp pile.

"Oh God, no!"

Cain raced over to his father, slipping and sliding on the extinguisher foam. Blood bubbled from between Mr. Williams' lips as his dazed brown eyes stared up at the ceiling. Water continued to trickle from the sprinklers, and while the cool liquid was such a relief, Mick couldn't even take the time to rejoice in it. Plus, it had reacted with the exposed, cut cables, causing even more fire to pop up. She scrambled to pick up the fire extinguisher, spraying down the surface of the control system until it was empty, and the sprinklers overhead had stopped. At the sound of Cain's soft sobs, she turned to face the others. Tommy crouched beside Mr. Williams as Cain scooped his father's head onto his lap.

"Cain," Tommy said, "don't move him. I don't think you're supposed to move him."

"Oh my God," Cain sobbed, tears streaming down his cheeks. They cut through the smoke and soot that had stained his mahogany skin. "What do you mean? What are we supposed to do? We can't leave him here. Can someone call 911?"

"We turned off electricity to the entire town," Tommy said, not unkindly or in a smart-aleck way, but in a calm tone of voice. "I don't know if the phones are going to work."

"If it's a landline, it'll work. We had to call the fire department once when a tree fell on my dad's car during a thunderstorm." Mick sprung to her feet. "I'm going to look for a breakroom or head back to the receptionist's desk. Maybe there's a corded phone there."

"Please hurry," Cain sobbed. His thumb brushed over the blood by his father's lips. Mr. Williams moaned in response, barely cognizant. Tremors coursed through the man's body, and it was unclear if he was heading into shock or experiencing a seizure. "Dad, hang on!"

Mick sprinted back out the doors. Her jaw dropped open when she saw that glass littered the hallways. CodeSkull had exploded every single light, suspending them in darkness. She kept one hand pressed against the wall and mentally tried to remember the twists and turns they had taken. *Right ... left ...* It helped when she turned a corner and skidded on some liquid—Tommy's gun must have been leaking as they were making their way to the mission control room. Another turn, and another, and soon, the sunlight was illuminating the way into the main lobby of the electrical plant. Glass glittered on the floor like confetti after a New Year's Eve ball, but she felt no joy, only a stomach-churning anxiety that nearly forced her to her knees.

She picked up the phone, surprised to hear a dial tone, and punched in the numbers to 911. As she clung to it, tremors overloaded her body. By the time that the operator answered, she was sobbing. She didn't know the address, but she told them that they were at the power plant. She begged for them to send an ambulance and said that someone had been electrocuted. When the dispatcher hung up, she stood by the door and waited until the ambulance came tearing down the road, another police vehicle in hot pursuit. As the EMTs and officers climbed out of their cars, she tearfully tried to explain to them what happened, but the words felt nonsensical as they left her mouth. She led them back through the dark hallways, over the trails of glass and water, until they reached Mr. Williams once more.

The EMTs immediately went to work, scooping the man up and placing him on the stretcher. As they wheeled him away, Cain attempted to follow, but an officer held him back, stating that no one could ride with him. Tears streamed down Cain's cheeks as he protested, at first politely, and then angrily, as his dad disappeared from the hallway.

"Let me see him!" Cain screamed, sobs wracking his body. "Let me see my dad! *DAD!*"

One of the officers raised their voice in irritation, and it was at that moment that Tommy wrapped his arms around Cain, squeezing him tight. Tommy's eyes uncomfortably scanned the officers, as though fearful. Mick also felt a sense of discomfort rumble her stomach, watching how they regarded Cain with such coldness.

She approached her friends as well and embraced them.

Chapter Eighteen

T ime stretched on for what felt like years, but by the time the cops dismissed them, it had only been an hour and a half. To her surprise, the cops hadn't called up her parents and demanded that they come to pick her up. They dismissed the three of them, ordering them to go home as soon as possible. As they left the building, one of the cops shook his head.

"It feels like the goddamn apocalypse," the man said.

Their water guns in hand, the children trudged out of the space, past other police officers that were starting to collect evidence. Little yellow placards highlighted various aspects of the crime scene: the destroyed receptionist's computer, the glass on the floor, the wet spots from where Tommy's water gun had leaked. Cain rubbed his eyes, the skin around them blotchy and dark, as though he hadn't slept in years. The scene felt so unusual to Mick. In every single movie she had ever watched, the heroes defeated the villain and walked away triumphant; laughing and jovial. Instead, she felt as low and grief-stricken as she did this morning.

They saved the town, but at the cost of so many lives—including, possibly, Cain's father.

"What the hell am I going to do without my dad?" Cain whispered.

Tommy squeezed his shoulder. "Cain, don't say that."

He tugged from his grasp. "He could be dead."

"The paramedics didn't say that," Tommy said. "Besides, if he had died on the scene, they would've taken him away in a body bag."

"Jesus Christ, Tommy," Mick muttered.

"I'm just trying to be helpful," Tommy said.

"Well, don't." Mick attempted to squeeze Cain's arm, but he recoiled from her touch. "Why don't we try to go to the hospital and see if we can find him? Once we get to the hospital, we can call your mom and let her know what's going on."

If the cops hadn't called her already. Mick didn't think that they had. They seemed all over the place. In a way she couldn't blame them, as with the number of accidents today, they had to be scrambling all over the place. Prior to today, the worst thing that had ever happened to Wildwood was when a rogue black bear had broken into the ice cream parlor and ate two weeks worth of rainbow sherbet.

Cain kicked at a crumbling chunk of asphalt in the parking lot. He didn't say a word as they walked the rest of the way to his car. Never had she seen anyone look so defeated. But what was she supposed to say? That it was all going to be okay? She didn't think so. To put it bluntly, Mr. Williams had been lit up like a Christmas tree. He had been shocked so badly that she had seen the shadow of his bones through his skin. The fact that he wasn't burnt to a crisp was a miracle in itself, but Mick didn't think that anyone could walk away from that without some serious injuries. It terrified her to think that that could have been her, or Tommy, or Cain.

And it wounded her deeply to realize that was what Tanner had experienced.

They climbed into the car, and each of them shut their doors. Cain made no move to put his key in the ignition. Tears welled in his eyes again and he punched the steering wheel, swearing. *"FUCK!"* He screamed louder, the rawness of his grief reverberating in their ears. *"FUCK!"* He continued to punch and beat the steering wheel and roof of his car, until finally his sobs consumed him once more, and he leaned over the dash, crying until he was completely breathless.

"Your dad is a hero," Tommy whispered, rubbing his shoulder. "And he believed in you."

Mick blinked back the tears rising in her own eyes. Cain moaned, incoherent, as though he was protesting against what Tommy said. But the boy repeated it, his voice as gentle as the first time.

"He saved our lives, Cain," Mick whispered. "Your dad saved our lives because he wanted to."

"Why don't we do what Mick suggested?" Tommy said. "We can try to go to the hospital and check on your dad. Give all of our parents a call."

"Okay," Cain whispered, the way a kindergartener would share a secret with a friend. At this moment, he finally turned the key in the ignition, and the car sputtered to life. "But I don't know how to get to the hospital."

"I think I do?" Tommy said. "My mom works the night shift as a nurse sometimes, and my dad would have to bring her lunch, so I'd tag along with him. I think we have to go around Wildwood Lake and we'll be there."

Cain nodded. They buckled their seatbelts and then slowly proceeded past the chaos of flashing lights, onto the main roadway. Mick rolled down the windows and felt the cool breeze on her face. They drove slowly this time, and as they progressed along their journey, Mick felt less dreadful, and more relaxed. The tension that had seeped its way into her aching shoulders was now ebbing. She rolled down the window more and let the wind comb its fingers through her hair.

"Cain," she said, "you remember that girl you had on the wall of your bedroom?"

He smirked at her in the rearview mirror, wiping at his eyes. "Poly Styrene?"

"Yeah. She's in a band, right?"

"Punk band. You want to give her a listen?"

Mick nodded. "Yeah. She seems cool."

Tommy cracked open the center console, sifting through the array of CDs. *Ok, Computer, Nevermind,*

Out of Time, and *Dirt,* before landing on the albums *Conscious Consumer* and *Germfree Adolescents.*

"That one first," Cain said. "We gotta get y'all started on your music education."

As "Identity" echoed through the speakers, Mick counted the number of trees that they passed by. Tommy, also knowledgeable about music, chatted with Cain about which R.E.M. album they liked best and if ACDC was overrated. Little by little, the despair that had overcome Cain was fading away. As the lake inched closer in view and the sun set lower on the horizon, any symptom of the tragedy they experienced had evaporated like smoke after a fire.

That is, until Mick spotted the green sparks emanating from one power line.

Chapter Nineteen

She had to rub her eyes when she spotted it. *What?* She saw the green sparks, licking and lapping the surface of the dusky early-night air like a bunch of clueless moths. Again she scrubbed, as though the sparks themselves were stuck in her lashes, but still, they persisted. She didn't have to say anything. Cain swerved the car over to the right shoulder.

"What the hell?" Tommy whispered, staring up at it.

Suddenly, the sparks stopped. The three exchanged looks.

"They didn't get the power plant back up and running, did they?"

"I don't ..." Cain trailed off, flabbergasted. "I don't know. I didn't see anyone from the power plant come back in; I only saw all the cops."

"And I don't see any other sparks," Mick said, scanning the entire stretch of road. Nothing.

"Well ..." Cain gritted his teeth and threw open his door.

"Cain!" Tommy cried out, also exiting the vehicle. "Wait a second!"

"No!" Cain shouted, spinning around to face him. "This shithead has chased us around all day, and I'm sick of it!"

He wrenched his water gun from the car, spinning around to face the powerline. Mick grabbed her gun and exited the vehicle as well, standing alongside him. Tommy shook his head, shaking his.

"I'm out, guys," he said. "What do I do?"

"Hang tight," Cain said, lifting his gun. "We're going to check this out."

Tommy whimpered wordlessly in response, all bravery and capability evaporating at the realization that they might be facing their foe once more. Mick's eyes flickered back and forth from one end of the road to the other. No green sparks. Nothing tingling. She looked down the road, in the supposed direction of the hospital. She noticed that there was a streetlight at the corner of this road and the adjacent one—it wasn't even on. But then again, was it late enough for the streetlights to come on? She knew it was after dinnertime, but she didn't think that the lights in the city came on at any particular time.

The wooden pole of the power line groaned as they approached. The thing was archaic; splintered in parts, and tilted backwards, as though ready to fall back into the lake below. Mick watched, jaw slack, as the cables snapped away from the power line and stretched towards them like greedy fingers.

"Goddamn it!" Cain roared. "Why won't you die!?"

He tucked and rolled as one of the cables attempted to strike him over the head, landing in the dirt. They jumped back as green sparks shot out of its frayed ends. The demon had definitely been weakened, and it clearly had nowhere to run, but that didn't mean it was going down without another fight. The two retreated from the powerline, pressing up against the car.

"What the hell are we going to do?" Tommy cried out. "If they turn the power plant back on, it's going to keep killing people. It'll be smart enough to not let us get that close again."

"I don't know, Tommy!" Cain snapped. "Let me think!"

CodeSkull's cables slapped against the ground, eager and happy like a wagging Labrador's tail. Spikes of electrical current coursed underneath them. Despair clenched around Mick's stomach and this time, when she felt the bile coming up the back of her throat, she didn't resist the urge to hold it down. She spewed into the roadside ditch, coughing up what little she had eaten at Taco Bell.

"Ew," Tommy said.

"I'm about to throw up," Cain said, his eyebrows knitting together in righteous fury. "This thing almost killed my dad and it *still* escaped the facility? It knew where we were going to go?"

"I don't think now's the time to ask why a demon is so much smarter than us," Tommy said. "I'm more concerned about how we're going to keep ourselves from dying. Should we run over to the lake and refill our guns?"

"The water's not going to work," Cain said, shaking his near-empty gun. The feeble amount of water sloshed around inside. "We already know that it'll barely hold him back, and by the time that we refill our guns, they could turn the power plant back on, and then we're all screwed. He'll follow us to the hospital and finish the job."

Wiping away the last traces of puke, Mick examined their options, her eyes flickering between the car and the pole. If the power plant was still off, which she guessed that it was, then CodeSkull couldn't run from them right now. And even though blasting him with their guns wouldn't effectively kill him, well, an entire body of water probably could, right? She stared at the decrepit pole, noting how it was tilted backwards. If something were to hit it hard and fast, it could potentially snap off its base and roll into the water.

As Tommy and Cain continued to argue about what to do next, Mick let her crazy idea take a hold of her. She felt almost possessed when she pushed past Cain and climbed into the driver's seat, locking the doors and windows, then buckling her seatbelt. Rather than react with panic, Cain rolled his eyes.

"Girl, why're you bugging? Get out of there."

Mick shook her head. She rolled down the window and passed him his collection of CDs. "I'm going to ram him."

"*WHAT?*" the boys shrieked.

Mick's fingers gripped the steering wheel. Never in her life had something felt simultaneously so strange, but so right. She stared up into Cain's face, knowing that she had little time left.

"Tell your dad I hope he feels better."

And then she gunned it.

Chapter Twenty

Once, when she was nine, Mick had spent a few weeks out on her grandfather's farm in Wisconsin. He had let her sit on his lap and drive the tractor, which could only go 15 miles an hour. Flying down the road at 70 mph, the cool wind whipping her face, she realized how little that experience prepared her for this. Once she reached the end of the road, she screeched to a stop, tires skidding across the dusty road. In the distance, Cain and Tommy were little ants, their thread-thin arms waving above their heads in a desperate attempt to make her stop.

But like Cain, Mick was tired of running. Tired of being afraid. Tired of feeling like her whole world was going to go up in flames at any moment. Nothing was going to stop her from putting this demon in the ground—or at the bottom of a lake.

Even if it meant sacrificing herself, at least her friends would live.

She adjusted the wheels, aiming it directly at the powerline. Checked her rear and side view mirrors to make sure no one was coming.

"This one's for you, Tanner."

Mick lifted her foot and slammed down on the gas pedal. *25... 30... 45...* The odometer climbed as much as Mick's heart rate did, till she could feel it almost leaping out of her chest. Tommy and Cain screamed for her to stop, but she didn't. The road dipped into the ditch, but the car miraculously soared over it, its massive force colliding against the pole with a thunderous boom. Green light surrounded her, and she felt as though she was caught in the middle of an exploding star. The air bags inflated and collided with her face, and through her muffled screams, she pushed them down. All over, she felt as though she was being stabbed by thousands of tiny little wasps. The powerline toppled backwards—crashing into the water.

And the car fell into the water with it.

Mick gulped down air and immediately tugged on the seatbelt, trying to free herself. The car and the powerline were sinking into the water. Through the windshield, she saw that CodeSkull was fading fast, his green glow dissipating into the inky waters. Mick gulped down another breath as she watched the water flood the car, sinking it faster. She tugged on the seatbelt again but couldn't break free.

She was going to drown if she didn't find a way to cut herself free.

Whimpering, Mick fumbled through the car in search of something, *anything* that could help her. She popped open the dash, only to discover fistfuls of papers. Popped open the center console, emptied of its CD treasures, with nothing more to be found. She attempted to pull on the seatbelt and lengthen it, hoping that she could wriggle herself out from underneath it. The water was now halfway through the car, and its front end tipped downwards, plunging below the murky waters. Just as Mick gulped down her last breath of air, she spotted it on the floor of the car.

Cain's switchblade.

She leaned forward, the murky waters obscuring her vision, and she grasped the blade, managing to snap it open. Through blurry eyes, she started to slice through the seatbelt that had coiled around her lap. The fibers began to sever, little by little, but she was so tired that she didn't know how much longer she could keep going. Her lungs were so strained she felt as though they would burst open like a balloon. Finally, she sliced through, severing the fabric in half. Turning to look out the open window, she could see the forest of algae that stretched out before her. Above, the surface seemed so far away. She didn't think that Wildwood Lake was that deep, but they were continuing to sink, and the light was fading.

Now freed from the seatbelt's clutches, Mick kicked her way out the open window, brushing past slimy strands of algae and kicking towards the surface. Her lungs choked on the lack of air, and bubbles escaped her mouth. The average person could only hold their breath for 30-90 seconds, and by some miracle, she had far surpassed that. By now, she was existing on borrowed time—maybe time that Tanner had bought for her. Mick kicked and kicked and pushed through the layers and layers of water that threatened to crush her.

Then she felt something coil around her leg and pull her down. A warbled scream let her mouth, bubbles flying in front of her face. Her head was beginning to pound from the lack of oxygen. She stared down to see the feeble cables of CodeSkull's powerline stretching out towards her. Using the switchblade, she slashed through the water and at her ankle, freeing herself from the demon's clutches. She kicked backwards, keeping her eyes on CodeSkull's powerline and the car as it faded into the darkness.

Her vision clouded. She felt as though a thousand holes had been torn within her chest and she was bleeding from every orifice. The pressure in her head built to the point where she felt like her brain would explode from the inside out. Black spots danced in front of her vision as her strength faded, but somehow, she was not panicked. In fact, she could feel a cool calmness wash over her as the world around her faded.

Even if she had failed, she would see Tanner again soon enough.

Chapter Twenty-One

"One, two, three!"

Something punched Mick's chest, and she bolted back to life, her eyes springing open and water exploding from the back of her throat. Someone's hands pulled back her hair as she twisted to the side and gagged, dry-heaving up all the water that had seeped its way into her stomach. Her pounding headache had returned, and her chest felt as though it was burning—she figured that with that car accident, she had probably bruised a few ribs.

As the world came into focus around her and she wiped the water from her mouth, she looked over at Cain and Tommy, whose panicked faces had broken into smiles of relief. But Mick's stomach could only churn. *Wait a minute.* Someone had performed CPR on her. Someone had performed—

"Oh my God, Tommy Perlaza, please don't tell me that you were the one who gave me my first kiss."

"It doesn't count," Cain told her as Tommy scoffed and haughtily told her, "You're fricking *welcome,* okay?"

"Tommy," Mick gasped, sucking air into her wounded lungs, "I'm going to kill you!"

"As gracious and grateful as ever," Tommy replied coolly, rising to his feet. It was Cain who had to help Mick up off the ground. "And by the way, I should kill you for performing a stunt like that. I knew you were a depressed-ass person, but I didn't think you were suicidal."

"You saved us," Cain murmured, smiling from ear to ear. "You destroyed my car, but you saved us."

"Any time," Mick replied, belching up more water.

The boys made noises of disgust. Cain even tried to peel himself away from her but her shaking knees buckled underneath her, and she almost dropped back onto the ground. Cain lifted her once more, slinging her arm around his shoulder. Gazing down at her body, she realized that she was covered in a variety of red and raw burns. Blood trickled down her legs and arms. What she had thought were wasp stings must've been little electrical sparks from the powerline's cables. Truly, it was a miracle she wasn't dead.

"Hospital's that way. Let's hop to it," Cain urged, inching her forward.

Tommy stood at the water's edge, gazing at the murky waters. "Do we think he's gone?"

"Well, to be safe, no one should ever go swimming in that lake again," Cain chirped. "Can you get my CDs?"

Chapter Twenty-Two

Because nothing could ever be that easy, Cain, Mick, and Tommy had hobbled for about a mile down the road before a truck passed by them and skidded to a halt. It ended up being Mr. Reade, Tanner's dad.

"Michelle Olivia Daniels!" he gasped as he rolled down his window. "Do you have *any* idea how much trouble you're in?" His eyes skimmed over her, and his anger quickly shifted from her to the boys. "What have you monsters done to her?!"

"Chill, chill," Cain called out. "She got hurt. We're taking her to the hospital. Can you give us a ride?"

"Mr. Reade," Mick mumbled, dazed from exhaustion. "What are you doing here?"

"What do you mean, what am I doing here?" he demanded, throwing open his door. He scrambled down the lift and opened the passenger door, urging the boys to slide her in. "You two, hop in the back. Mick, you went *missing*. Your parents called us worried sick because you took off with some *boy* this morning and didn't come back."

"We were a little busy," Mick replied, sleepily. "We got Taco Bell."

"Uh huh," Mr. Reade snapped, shutting the passenger door. As he climbed back in the driver's seat, Mick saw his expression soften, and the man's eyes well with tears.

"Mr. Reade?"

"I just lost my daughter," he whispered, wiping the tears from his eyes. "And she ... she loved you so much. To think that you'd be gone, too, is ..."

He shook his head, expelling the thought from his mind as he shifted the truck in gear. Mick thought that was a good thing. After all, she had almost died countless times today. The truck rolled down the road in silence, and Mick couldn't even hear Tommy or Cain talking as they usually did. Finally at ease, she allowed herself to drift away once more.

Only to wake up to the sting of a needle.

"Ow!" Mick cried out.

She glanced down at her wounded arm to see that a nurse had inserted the IV drip. She was laying in a hospital bed, in a fresh clean gown, her body dry. A scratchy-ass blanket covered her legs and torso. She lifted it up, looking at the gauze and bandages that had wrapped their way around the lower half of her body. Clearly she had been out for some time. She stared around her small hospital room, trying to take everything in. The bleach white lights above her were doing nothing for her pounding head.

Huh.

She really hoped she didn't have a concussion.

"Sorry about that!" the nurse chirped. Smokey blue eyeshadow highlighted the natural color of her irises. "Just a little pinch!"

"What are you putting in me? Drugs? Is it drugs?"

The nurse pouted in disapproval. "It's an IV drip. It's got fluids. You're extremely dehydrated."

Mick blinked. "I almost drowned."

"Well, maybe you should've kept some of that water in your system," the nurse replied, all sweetness gone. She left the room in a whirl. Shortly after, Tommy and Cain came stumbling through the door, their arms full of vending machine snacks.

"Yo!" Cain said, a smile breaking across his face. "There she is!"

"Mr. Reade left, but he called your parents. They're on their way here," Tommy said. "My mom's also on shift right now, and she said she'll swing by to check on us in a bit."

They dumped the crinkly bags into her lap, and she spluttered with laughter. Cracker Jacks, Famous Amos, Funyons, and Cheetos. Mick had longed for a junk food heaven but never thought that one would be brought to her.

"I woke up to a needle in my arm," Mick said, cracking open a bag of Cheetos. "Not something I'd recommend."

"You've been through worse today, champ," Cain replied, tearing into his own bag of chips. He cracked open a soda and plopped down in a chair. "I feel like a needle in your arm is the least of your worries."

"Cain, do you know what's going on with your dad?"

A dark expression clouded Cain's eyes. "He's apparently in a medically induced coma. We're waiting to see if he comes out of it."

"Oh no ..." Mick whispered. "I'm so sorry."

"Hey, he's alive, and that's all that matters right now. But from what the doctor told me and my mom, he's got a long road to recovery ahead of him. Not to mention all the shit that happened to our house, and my car." His eyes bulged out of his head. "I've never heard my mama scream like that in all my life. I would pay any amount of money to forget it."

"If you need some help cleaning the place up, I got you," Tommy offered.

Cain smirked. "Thanks Tommy, but I don't think you can help us clean up severe structural damage."

"Probably not, no. But I'm willing to try."

"Thanks," Cain said, and then looked at Mick again. "The power plant came back online and nothing's happened. No green sparks have chased us here. So I would say that you saved the day."

"Fricking *finally*," Mick groaned, throwing her head back against the pillow. "They make defeating evil look *so* much easier in the movies."

"Next time we come across some terrifying evil from the great beyond, I really hope it's something that I can beat with a stick." Tommy stacked and clenched his fists together as though he was holding a sword. "I gotta get some of this anger out of my system."

"No," Cain groaned. "No more demons or dealing with the occult for me. I've had more than enough."

"Hey, how'd they let you guys in here, by the way? I thought hospitals only allowed visitors for family."

"Oh they don't know that we're in here," Tommy said, crunching down on a Funyon. "The hospital is *swamped*. It is packed with people. CodeSkull messed up a bunch of intersections across town, so a lot of people got into accidents. And the ER is full of people who were shocked by one thing or another today. You think your burns look bad? There's one dude whose entire face looks like one blister, ripe for popping—"

"—The town has had one *mondo* bad day," Cain interjected. "I'm glad that we were able to stop the damn thing from hunting down and killing literally everyone. It felt like we were living in *Hard Target*."

"What?" Tommy asked.

"Dude, I'm begging you to watch a movie that's not animated."

Tommy pressed his lips together as though trying to suppress a smirk. "Maybe you could give me a list of movies to watch sometime, and I'll take you up on that."

"I'd like that." Cain smiled.

At that moment, a woman entered the doorway, but she wasn't a nurse. She was dressed in business professional clothing and had glamorous short hair that cropped around her ears. She stared at Mick for a second before looking down at Cain.

"Micah," she said, "it's time to go for the night."

"Oh," Cain said, sitting upright. Although quiet, the shock was palpable in his voice.

Suddenly it felt like they were all dealing with the melancholy end of an epic slumber party. The three of them stared at each other, not knowing what to say. Cain made no effort to leave his chair. Nervousness swirled in Mick's stomach like a twisted ice cream cone. Now that this was over, would Cain—older, wiser, absolutely cooler Cain—want to hang out with them again? Would he even talk to them after this? Heck, would Tommy talk to her after this?

Confused by the silence, Mrs. Williams arched a brow and stepped into the room. She looked at Mick with an expression of curiosity.

"You must be ... Mick, right?" she asked, wincing as though she had made a mistake.

"Mick!" She nodded. "Yep. Technically it's Michelle but I don't go by that. Only Mickey or Mick. Preferably Mick."

Wow, she was babbling. Clearly she'd hit her head harder than she had anticipated.

"Mick. Cain tells me that you were the one who called 911 for my husband and brought the paramedics to them. Is that so?" Mrs. Williams asked.

Mick nodded. In a few quick strides, Mrs. Williams had cleared the distance between them. She scooped Mick's hands into hers and squeezed them, tears springing to her eyes.

"Thank you," she whispered. "You saved his life. They're saying that some of the wires were faulty and that led to all these explosions earlier today, and that's why he had to shut down the power plant. You and my husband are both heroes."

Blood rushed into Mick's cheeks. "Uh, y-you're welcome. I'm uh, glad I could help."

"When all this is over," Mrs. Williams said, releasing her hands, "and my beautiful house isn't in disarray, I'd love to have you over for dinner. I insist."

"S-sure," Mick stammered. "I'd love that."

"Great. Well ..." Mrs. Williams glanced over at Cain, who remained in his seat, stricken with that same stupefied expression. "Don't give me that look, son. We'll be back tomorrow."

Sheepishly, Cain rose to his feet. He glanced at Tommy and Mick, offering them a small smile. "I guess I'll see y'all ..."

"Tomorrow!" Tommy chimed in, overeager. "I'll be back tomorrow too."

Mick groaned, although she felt relieved. "Oh God."

Cain chuckled and shook his head as he exited the room along with his mother. Now that he was gone, it felt like the weight of everything that they had been through today hit Mick with the force of ten trucks. She wiped at her eyes as she cracked open a now-lukewarm can of Coke.

"Do you know how long they said I'd be here?" Mick asked him.

Tommy shook his head. "No, but I do know that you have bruised ribs, sprained both your ankles, and have a possible concussion. We probably shouldn't have let you go back to sleep in the truck. Oops."

"I forgive you."

"Thanks." Tommy chuckled, now moving to occupy the seat that Cain had left. "I'll hang with you until your parents get here. My mom said I needed to call my dad when I was ready to go home."

"Okay." Mick curled her body into a tight ball beneath her uncomfortable blanket. "Thanks."

"No problem." Tommy smiled as he crunched into another Funyon. "So, um ... Mr. Reade says that Tanner's funeral's going to be on Saturday. My mom wanted me to ask you if you wanted to be picked up or if your parents were planning on taking you. Or we could take you home. She said that we could go get ice cream afterwards or something."

"A funeral, and then ice cream?" Mick arched a brow.

"It doesn't have to be ice cream. I just think that ..." He took a deep breath. "I don't know. Maybe you won't want to go home when it's over. And if you don't, the offer's open. You can come over and hang out. Unless you're planning on hanging out with someone else."

Mick licked the Cheetos dust off her fingers. "No, I don't think I will. Like I said, she was …"

"She was not your only friend. I don't know what happened with Louise and Peggy last year, but I think if we've proven anything today, it's that you've got at least two more people you can count on. What happened, anyways? You never finished that story."

"You know Brandon Loudermilk? We were lab partners last year, and it turns out that he liked me. But Peggy likes him, so she thought that I was 'stealing' him from her. She went around the entire school and told everyone that I was a boyfriend-stealing skank. Mind you, he was never her boyfriend."

"*Loudermilk?* She likes *Loudermilk?* The dude on the basketball team with the overbite and greasy hair? I mean, I'm no Casanova, but—"

"—Yeah, I don't like Brandon, either," Mick interjected. "Tanner was the only one who saw the bullshit for what it was and stuck by me. She was a true friend."

Tommy smiled. "You are, too." He closed his eyes and tilted his head to look up at the ceiling, as though basking in rays of sunlight, instead of ugly fluorescent lighting. "I'm sure that she's up there in her own personal heaven with twenty-three Liu Kangs and she's thrilled that you avenged her."

"I hope you're right," Mick whispered.

"Girl, I know I'm right." Tommy rolled his eyes.

At that moment, two more people squeezed into the doorway. Mick found herself staring at her parents. Instantaneously, her mother burst into tears and flung herself on her bed, crushing the various bags of potato chips underneath her. Her dad was more awkward, shuffling into the room and hovering by the bedside, unsure of what to do or say. Tommy smiled, stood up, and quietly slunk from the room like a cat. He didn't bother to say goodbye.

She knew that she'd see him tomorrow.

Chapter Twenty-Three

"What up, dorks?"

Mick turned away from the pinball game to see Cain approaching. He was dressed in his normal getup, his nametag from Flicks Forever still pinned to his chest. The store had managed to salvage some of its VHS tapes and was leasing a temporary location nearby until the old building was rebuilt. Tommy didn't bother to look away from the pinball game, spamming the buttons for the paddles and launching the little steel ball into orbit once more.

"Nothing much," Mick said. "'Sup with you? How was work?"

"Boring," Cain replied. "And I don't know why this one third grader keeps checking out *The Little Mermaid* over and over again. Like, at that point, just buy it on VHS. I don't even want to think about how much her parents have spent on *The Little Mermaid*."

Tommy groaned as the steel ball shot between the paddles. "Ugh, that was my last ball."

"Oh no," Cain said. "Do you hear that, Mick? He doesn't have any balls."

Mick giggled as Tommy elbowed Cain in the stomach. The older boy staggered backwards from the blow, laughing.

"Where are we headed to tonight, y'all?" He dangled the keys to his new car from his fingers. As it turns out, Cain had a cousin that was moving to New York City, so he used the insurance money from losing his old car to buy that one off of her.

"Actually, uh, we didn't want to head out for awhile. Mick was waiting for the Dig Dug game to free up. She was going to try to beat her old score."

Mick glanced over at the arcade machine, whose last occupant had now wandered away. She hadn't played Dig Dug since her and Tanner had been here last. Nearly a month later, and with Labor Day right around the corner, she still didn't feel ready, but with the boys by her side, she screwed up some of her courage. The three of them drifted over to Dig Dug. Mick fumbled with the quarters in her pocket and loaded one into the machine.

It had begun. The little 8-bit intro music played as Mick's character assumed its position in the center of the dirt maze. Navigating the labyrinth, Mick's confidence grew, and with each little monster that she exploded, her score climbed higher and higher. Cain and Tommy cheered her on, but not loud enough to distract her—they knew exactly how deeply she'd have to concentrate to beat her score. She surpassed level after level, spamming buttons and twisting the joystick with expert finesse. Hundreds of points scored turned into thousands and then tens of thousands. Climbed into the hundreds of thousands. At some point the boys took bathroom breaks. An hour in, she lost her first life. But the loss did not send her spiraling into despair.

Instead, it made her bloodthirsty.

Mick approached her next levels more ruthless than before. She hunted down the monsters as they scrambled to flee the screen, securing extra lives with each 20,000 points she earned. By now she was drenched in sweat, and a sudden heat overwhelmed her. She realized that she was surrounded on all sides by avid spectators. At first their whispers shook her concentration, but she squared her shoulders, sinking deeper into her mission. Her score climbed higher, and higher, until finally, there it was:

900,000 points.

The best she had ever achieved.

"Keep going, Mick!" Tommy said, clapping his hands as she lost her next life. "You've got this!"

A few surrounding people continued to clap their hands and cheer for her. Admittedly, Mick had lost steam. At this point, she had been standing for nearly two hours straight, and the sweat underneath her armpits was starting to feel uncomfortable. Tommy offered her a cold can of Mountain Dew, and she pressed the can against her warm and swollen cheeks, exhaling a sigh of relief. Bashful, she waved to the surrounding people, and watched as her character's lives were picked off one by one by the enemies.

"You could've gone for longer if you wanted to," Cain said.

"Nah," Mick replied, cracking open the can. "I've got time to come back and do this again."

"Great!" He clapped his hands together. "Let's dip!"

"Dip-duh-dip-duh-dip," Tommy sang out, traipsing after their friend.

Mick followed, close behind, out into the parking lot, where Cain's new car, a shiny blue '94 Honda Civic, awaited them. As August slowly transitioned into September, the weather was becoming cooler. She shivered a bit as she climbed into the backseat of Cain's car. Tommy riding shotgun, because of course Tommy wanted to ride shotgun.

"Good goddamn," Cain said as he turned on the car. "It's almost seven thirty. How'd I convince y'all to let me stay in that dank-ass place until seven thirty?"

"There's not a lot of windows in Gearscore, so you don't really know that time is passing until you check a clock," Tommy said. "Honestly, it seems kinda like a fire hazard to not have windows, don't you think?"

"I'm starving," Cain said. "Luckily for us, my mom picked up a thirty dollar gift card from Applebee's."

"I was hoping that we could go to McDonald's," Tommy said. "They've got Hot Wheels in the Happy Meals this month. They're NASCAR themed."

"Tommy, did you not hear me? I have a gift card to Applebee's. We're going to Applebee's."

"Fine," Tommy sighed, as though the concept of being given free food was egregiously awful to him. "Mick, are you good with Applebee's?"

"Mick," Cain said, "please don't make me sit in the car with y'all while you hork down Happy Meals. I beg of you, spare what little dignity I have left. It's bad enough that I'm hanging out with fresh meat. Actually, y'all aren't even fresh meat yet, so that's worse."

"Applebee's sounds good to me," Mick said. "I can always get an Oreo shake."

"That's the spirit! Applebee's, it is!"

The car shifted into drive, and Cain popped in his latest alt rock CD: *Generation Swine* by Motley Crüe. Music vibrated through the car, and Mick smiled as Tommy and Cain launched into another one of their arguments—this time, it seemed to be about whether *Top Gun* was a good movie. Laughing to herself, Mick rolled down her window and felt the breeze caress her face.

The night called out to them.

Acknowledgements

Video games have been a part of my life for as long as I can remember. Honestly, I'm surprised it's taken me this long to write a story that's so deeply inspired by them. My love for those classic Scooby Doo films—you know, like *Zombie Island* or more accurately for this book, *Cyber Chase*—also influenced the creation of this story.

Special thanks to Joey Powell, my publisher, for taking a chance on this wild concept, and for designing the amazing cover, which brought each of the characters to life. I was so excited for the opportunity to write this book, and he's been supportive every step of the way. Thank you to Nico Bell for her infectious enthusiasm and hard work editing this book and correcting my many, *many* misplaced commas.

An additional thank you to Aurora and Bri, who beta read this story, and provided so much valuable feedback. I'm grateful to both of you for your friendship, endless support, and memes. I'm giggling now as I write this.

To the friends who helped me survive grade school and beyond: Elizabeth, Sabrina, and the inspiration for Tommy himself, Christian, thank you for showing up to my signings, for preordering, for sending pictures of my books at different stores and being my biggest champions. Life may have taken us all in different directions, but I'm glad that we're still in each other's lives.

Thank you to all the educators, librarians, and parents-of-readers who have picked up this book for their kids or students. Encouraging lifelong reading in kids will forever benefit them, and I'm so glad that you're taking the time to support and foster their love of reading. Honestly, it's hearing from folks like you directly at conventions and tabling events while doing the press tour for my last book *Haunting Melody* (a YA release for 16+ readers) that inspired me to write this book in the way that I did. You are your children's heroes.

Finally, an extra special thank you to you, reader. I wrote this book for kids like Mick, Tommy, and Cain—kids who at one point or another felt like outcasts. I definitely was more like Mick than I'd care to admit! If you see yourself in one of these characters, or maybe all of them, I want to commend you for your strength and remind you to look for the people who will get you. You will find them, even if it takes you a while. I hope that you had fun, and that you're not too scared to sleep with the lights off tonight! Please don't be afraid of your blender or household appliances. I promise this is a total work of fiction!

Just be a lil' suspicious if you ever pick up an old floppy disc, okay?

About the Author

Minnesota native Chloe Spencer (she/her) is an award winning writer, indie gamedev, and filmmaker. She is the author of multiple horror novellas, novels, and short stories. In her spare time she enjoys playing video games, trying her best at Pilates, and cuddling with her cats. She holds a BA in Journalism from the University of Oregon and an MFA in Film and Television from SCAD Atlanta.

Mick, Tommy, and Cain will return in

GHOST GLADIATOR

Coming 2021

9 781966 649700 4